COUNSEL
CULTURE

ALSO BY KIM HYE-JIN

Central Station

Concerning My Daughter

The Work of No. 9

Fire and My Autobiography

Eobi

A Life Called You

KIM HYE-JIN

COUNSEL CULTURE

a novel

Translated from the Korean by
Jamie Chang

RESTLESS BOOKS

NEW YORK • AMHERST

Translation copyright © 2024 Jamie Chang

Originally published as 경청 (Gyeongcheong) by 김혜진 (Kim Hye-jin) in Korea by Minumsa Publishing Co., Ltd. Published in arrangement with Kim Hye-jin c/o Minumsa Publishing Co., Ltd, and Casanovas & Lynch Literary Agency

First Restless Books paperback edition March 2024

Paperback ISBN: 9781632062321
Library of Congress Control Number: 2023945242

This book is published with the support of the Literature Translation Institute of Korea (LTI Korea).

This book is supported in part by an award from the National Endowment for the Arts.

This book is made possible by the New York State Council on the Arts with the support of Governor Kathy Hochul and the New York State Legislature.

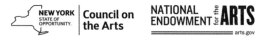

Cover design by Jonathan Yamakami
Designed and typeset by Tetragon, London
Cover photographs by Zixuan Fu and Arielle Allouche

Printed in the United States

1 3 5 7 9 10 8 6 4 2

RESTLESS BOOKS
NEW YORK · AMHERST
www.restlessbooks.org

COUNSEL CULTURE

To Mr. Seong-mok Lee:

Hello, it's Haesoo Lim.

It may surprise you to receive this letter. Or perhaps you've forgotten my name altogether. An event that's easily forgotten by one person remains indelible for another, even in death. Isn't it astonishing that the one who cannot forget dies on the inside while the one who has forgotten goes about their life as if nothing happened?

Then again, perhaps to live is to learn to do much worse.

Pretending to be alive. Living, but more or less dead. Looking at myself now, I see that these things are possible. I'm sure you can guess the reason why.

Even now, I can go on the internet and see the articles you wrote. The articles about me. How you could write these articles without the most basic fact-checking, I cannot understand.

Why my request that you take down the article—just a patchwork of rumors floating around—keeps being turned down, why you rebuffed this reasonable demand

Haesoo pauses here and puts down her pen. The smudge of ink on the back of her hand leaves a black mark on the bottom of the page. The letter is ruined. She has to start over. But she knows that it's not the ink stain that ruined it. It is simply not enough. This vocabulary, this polite, smooth language will not convey her message.

She looks down at the words she chose. Then she picks up the pen and strikes out the words *perhaps* and *indelible* and *dies on the inside. Cannot forget* becomes *will not forget. Name* becomes *existence*. But the cautious, unsure tone imbued in the letter does not lift.

These simple words and sentences cannot express the feelings that overwhelm her so often. They are not enough. Instead, something sharp and scorching. Something to keep the sparks burning.

She's always had a habit of hiding her feelings. There are moments she can't bear, of course, but they are generally tolerable, and she forgets easily. She has always thought herself to be in control of her emotions. That it is her own power and will that make this control possible. But now that everything seems impossible, she has to admit it was the circumstances built around her that made control possible.

Haesoo folds the letter in half, then again, puts it in her pocket, and leaves the house. It's the hour when people out for a late-night walk have gone home. In front of a store, a few drunk stragglers pass around a pack of cigarettes, their flushed faces illuminated in the headlights of passing cars.

She makes her way out of the narrow alley, crosses the four-lane street, and heads to the park. It's dark and deserted. Until a few years ago, this area was the battleground of run-down stall bars. At dusk, colorful strings of lights switched on and sliding glass doors covered with contact paper would be left open for customers all night long. The glimpses inside were slipshod, perverse, somewhat sad. This place was a harbor—all discarded things washed up here.

Now there is no trace of all that.

Now there are apartment buildings spaced out evenly, stores with plate-glass windows you can look into, spacious roads, clean sidewalks. People come and go as though they have forgotten what used to be here. But then again, those who know what this place used to be don't live here anymore.

She walks the long length of the park. In adequate stillness and gentle light, she tries to look for inner peace. Spring is near. She focuses on the air surrounding her. The shadows of the trees quiver faintly when the wind blows. The shadows, mere lines through winter, are slowly building their shape. In the next few months, they will begin to bulk up and grow.

A late-night walk can be beneficial in many ways.

During the day, when everything is exposed, people like to talk about exposed things. Perhaps it is only at night when visibility is low that people's terrifying curiosity takes a rest. She begins a second lap around the park, choosing the darker paths, then stops at the garbage can by the entrance. She removes the folded letter from her pocket and tears it over the bin. As if to discard her feelings there. As if to vow that she will never let these feelings seize her again.

When she returns to her street, she finds two neighbors arguing.

Why do you keep putting food out by my house? The voice comes from a woman's small frame with a stooped back.

Ma'am, this isn't by anything of yours. This is the street. Street's for everyone's use, answers the taller of the two silhouettes.

That's what I'm asking. Why are you leaving food out for cats in the street that everyone uses? Leave it by your own house if you like them so much. Why are you bothering people in this neighborhood?

When did I bother anyone? These cats need to eat, too. How am I bothering you by feeding cats? You're the one bothering me, ma'am.

One voice attacks, the other defends. One is a lance, the other a block. Neither is ready to yield.

A car drives by, blaring a hit song. The plaintive, mournful melody slowly fades as the car turns a corner. Haesoo presses close to an illegally parked truck. To reach her house, she has to pass the two people in confrontation, and one of them might notice her walking by. They might even talk to her. Ask her to take sides, ask her questions that put her in a difficult position. Say things she should not have to hear.

A few days earlier, Haesoo was subjected to just such an attack.

She was browsing the produce section plastered with signs that said BOGO, Unbeatable Prices, Everything Must Go. Someone stealing glances at Haesoo as she stood in front of the romaine and celery approached.

Aren't you Dr. Haesoo Lim? You are, right? It's so weird to see you at a place like this. Do you live around here?

The woman wore a blue cardigan with a yellow tote bag slung over one shoulder. The large pair of sunglasses she was wearing on her head seemed ready to slip off at any moment.

Haesoo did not respond, but the woman made eye contact with her as she added, This may not mean much to you, but I don't think what happened was entirely your fault. People talk, but they don't really know what they're talking about. They just like to talk. Don't mind them.

Haesoo smiled gently at the woman. Or rather, she tried to smile. She felt the muscles on her face tighten as if paralyzed.

Here's what I really think. Back when the articles were pouring out about you, you really should have taken a firmer stance. You need to be aggressive with people like that, or they won't shut up. If you give them the impression that you don't know what to do, they'll tear you apart. These people are incorrigible.

Haesoo fixed her eyes on the pyramid of lettuce. She had to get through this moment. If the head of lettuce delicately balanced on the top had not rolled off, if a few more had not gone down with it, causing an avalanche of lettuce heads and panic among the staff, she would have had to stand there and

7

listen to all these thoughtless comments the woman was pummeling her with until she decided she was done.

I'm not like these people, she thinks. I'm different from these people.

There are words that draw lines in the sand. Words that drive others away. Words meant to show one's moral superiority and sense of justice. All of these words are the same to Haesoo—they are a reminder of the past, proof that nothing has been forgotten, a warning that her name will come up again and again in this context. Perhaps she is self-conscious and indulging in victim mentality. But she doesn't want to get involved, whatever it is, whomever it's with. She doesn't want to be associated.

When she turns her head, a yellow creature dives and vanishes under the parked truck.

Haesoo follows a regimented routine.

She gets up at eight in the morning, does some light stretching in bed, brushes her teeth, and drinks a glass of water. Then she opens the windows and has a cup of coffee as she listens to the radio, usually programs that share little stories about the listeners' lives. She has a late breakfast before ten, then does chores around the house until noon. In the afternoon, time passes quickly. Two o'clock and three o'clock slip by in quick succession. Then comes evening.

Before dinner, she usually writes a letter. This is the most important task of her day. She begins each letter with *Hello*, then places carefully chosen words like stepping stones into a disorienting maze of expressions. When night falls, she takes the unfinished letter with her on a walk. She strolls around the park for about an hour, disposes of the scrupulously worded letter, and comes home relieved that another day has gone by.

Her days flow calmly and quietly, or so it seems on the surface. On the inside is brittle glass that breaks at the gentlest impact. Any damaged part cannot be returned to the way it was. She knows this to be true, but she cannot abandon hope that she will recover the inner self she had before.

An unattainable wish. An improbable dream.

This belief may be the reason Haesoo is able to maintain her disciplined routine.

At night, she sees that creature again on her way back from her walk. The yellow thing that hid under the truck. She squats, leans down. A cat is balled up under the truck. It looks at her, its eyes two gleaming lights in the darkness.

So, it's you. You're the reason people are fighting around here.

Haesoo mumbles to herself and extends a hand. The balled-up cat opens its jaw a little and makes a chary gesture. The cat is small. Not a kitten, but it doesn't seem fully grown either.

Here, kitty.

Haesoo gets closer to the ground and extends her hand again. She hears voices approach, then fade away. Two motorcycles zip past as if they're racing. Both ears flat against its head, the cat glances around in fear, maintaining a vigilant distance from Haesoo.

You're a scaredy cat, aren't you?

Haesoo is just about to get up when the cat cries. She ducks down and looks more closely. The cat cries again.

There is a red spot on the cat's forehead. Dried blood. Haesoo turns her head sideways and carefully studies the cat's wound. A red scab the size of a coin has turned dark, a white ring of infection spreading out. One of the cat's front paws is swollen as if it's wearing a boxing glove. When she leans in to take a closer look, the cat tucks its paw under its body.

At a nearby convenience store, Haesoo buys a carton of milk and a packet of chicken breast to ease the hunger of that small being. To save it from the cigarette butts, the plastic wrappers, all the garbage filling the darkness. Haesoo projects herself onto the cat and reverts to self-pity again.

She sees her own reality in the cat huddled under the truck and is reminded of her own misfortune. How easy it is to see her sadness, anger, and injury in an alley cat that has nothing to do with her. The self-pity she feels seems boundless.

When she returns, the cat is gone. She waits for a long while, but the cat has seen through her intentions. Haesoo goes home and puts the milk and chicken in the fridge.

Haesoo has no complaints about her routine. She has stuck to it for almost a year.

But she knows she is not suited for a monotonous life. She knows better than anyone that she will not be able to settle for boredom. All the things she wanted from life. She never imagined it would be reduced to such a bland, unremarkable thing.

Her life has become just another life. It might as well be someone else's. She is no longer the master of it.

The next evening, Haesoo sees the cat again. It peers out from under the truck, then darts back underneath when it sees her coming. She approaches slowly, pours the milk into a paper cup, and offers the chicken breast whole.

Go on. Come have a bite, she gently encourages the cat, but it does not move. Its bright, gleaming eyes track her movement. Is this unrelenting guardedness toward others an innate quality? Or was it learned out of necessity? Whatever it is, it doesn't change the fact that it makes for a lonely, tiring life. Feeling herself slip into self-pity, Haesoo gathers herself and takes a step back.

The cat stretches its neck and sniffs at her offerings.

Uh, hello, a voice calls to Haesoo. She turns to find a little girl standing behind her. She is maybe too big to be a little girl, actually—elementary school? Middle school? Haesoo tries to guess as the two of them make eye contact.

I don't think the cat can eat that thing whole. Cats have small mouths. Isn't that chicken breast? He had cat food just now.

Do you know this cat?

When Haesoo gets up, the girl seems smaller.

She transfers a large duffle bag to her opposite shoulder and lightly hops in place. This cat? I know him. Is that chicken breast for people to eat? You can't give cats people food. It's seasoned, which is bad for cats' kidneys.

Is that right? Haesoo says, glancing at the murky-white piece of chicken on the ground. It might have looked tasty on a plate, but here it seems out of place. Haesoo isn't sure if she should pick up the meat or leave it there. The girl ducks down to inspect it for herself. The duffle bag tips forward, rattling its contents.

Oh, this is fine. It's not seasoned. I eat this sometimes, too. It tastes like nothing, the child says. She sits down and starts fishing around in her bag. Her movements are ungainly and abrupt, heedless and natural. Unmindful of others. This disarms Haesoo for a moment.

When you see him next time, why don't you give him one of these? He loves them.

What's this?

Churu. It's a cat treat. If you get it on your hand, it stinks really bad.

A black sedan honks as it drives by. Haesoo and the girl press close to the truck. There is a sheen of sweat on the girl's face. A sour smell of sweat wafts up from her body, a smell one would expect from someone who has endured a day of hard labor. Haesoo's gaze cautiously takes in the child's sports socks, the sports band on one wrist, the hair pulled into a tight ponytail.

Tear this part a little bit and squeeze. He won't come to you, so you have to squeeze it on the ground.

Haesoo takes a stick of Churu from the child. This is the longest conversation she has ever had with anyone from this neighborhood. She has acquaintances here, but the few she knows have forgotten how to have a conversation with her. They judge and argue. They warn and pontificate. They seem to enjoy keeping her locked in her past.

Cats like these treats, huh? How much do I owe you? Haesoo searches her purse.

The child answers coolly, You don't have to pay. I got it from some lady. Don't forget to give it to the cat when you see him next time. The child points under the truck. The cat has emerged and laps at the milk. Its swollen paw dangles awkwardly, but its balance on three legs is perfectly steady. Haesoo and the child watch intently.

Do you see that? The front paw? It's much better now. A few weeks ago, it was really swollen. He couldn't walk very well, the girl says.

Wary, the cat again disappears under the truck. Haesoo isn't sure why the child is telling her all this. She doesn't understand why she is having a conversation with a child she just met.

But the worst is over, the girl is saying. At least that's what the lady who feeds the cats says. She said the cat is stronger than people think. He fought off the infection well. She said street cats are smarter and braver than people think.

Haesoo likes the sound of that. She takes another look under the truck and the cat carefully peers back. Haesoo sees the cat in a different light now. She asks the girl a few more questions. When does the cat usually appear? Where does he eat? Who are the people that feed the cat? How old is he? When did he get injured? And so on. The child answers the questions dutifully. But when her cell phone rings, she stops.

I have to go now, she says.

What's your name?

It's Turnip. I named him myself, the girl answers, and turns around. Haesoo was asking the child, not the cat. But she nods in response anyway. When the child has made her way down the street, Haesoo shouts, Do you know how the cat hurt himself?

People are always surprised when I tell them I'm in the fourth grade! the girl shouts back. But I really am! She crosses the street where cars come and go, then vanishes.

Dear Juhyun,

I tried calling a few times, but I guess you weren't available. How are you? I'm doing okay. I'm trying to, at least. And I know that it's important that I make the effort. You know what I mean?

I'm sure you noticed I was on edge the last time we saw each

14

other. I couldn't help it. I was out of my mind. I remember you telling me that it would pass soon. That I just have to get through it. That I don't have to make an even bigger mess of things.

I knew you were just looking out for me, but I hated hearing it at the time. It sounded like a warning that a bigger mess was coming. I was frightened. I didn't want anyone to see that, so I screamed. I abused everyone—especially those closest to me.

That doesn't justify what I said to you. I don't know why I suddenly brought it up. I asked you if you were enjoying my misery. I said, How's it feel to have a front-row seat to this trainwreck? Then I brought up an unhappy period from your past and threw it in your face. *Threw it in your face* is exactly the expression. I can't believe how low I stooped.

You watched as I rambled on like a crazy person until you left. I wonder what was going through your mind. Maybe that was the moment our relationship ended. I did not shut up until I heard you leave and close the front door behind you. I finally shut up because tears poured out and I couldn't speak. I remember wailing for a long time, grieving for the things I lost, for the things I would lose in the days to come. Grieving for my life that would plummet without end.

I did not realize at the time that you were one of the most important things I would lose. That did not even occur to

Haesoo stops and reads it from the beginning. She reads the letter over and over, until she can admit that the words she has written are an unflagging attempt at self-deception.

Does Haesoo want to reconcile with Juhyun? Is she trying to say she's sorry? No, Haesoo knows that it's neither. She wants to explain why she did what she did. She wants to convince Juhyun that she had no choice. But this letter is another failure.

On her nightly walk back from disposing of the letter, she idles by the truck. Since she gave Turnip the Churu she got from the girl, she has bought a few more. In her pocket are three packets of Churu, each with slightly different ingredients and flavors.

Haesoo has never taken an interest in animals before now.

For many years, she thought herself to be a competent therapist. As a therapist, she only dealt with people. With the emotions people feel, with feelings that overwhelm them. Because Haesoo believed that she had complete control over her own emotions, she was able to offer decisive advice to those who were controlled by their feelings and moods. There was no place for animals or plants in her life—just people. A life bursting only with human things. A perfectly human life?

Haesoo returns from her runaway train of thought and looks around. It takes a while, but she spots Turnip. He isn't under the illegally parked truck, but up on the wall looking down on the cars.

Little face, pink button of a nose, disproportionately large and pointy ears, sharp claws hidden in tiny paws. A strip of yellow fur begins above the eyes, draws a path down the back, and wraps around the tail.

That isn't all Haesoo has learned about Turnip.

Haesoo takes a Churu from her pocket and slowly approaches. Turnip's gaze darts around, as if he cannot decide whether to run or stay. The indecision is a positive sign. Turnip stays put even as Haesoo comes close.

Do you want a treat? Look. You like this, don't you?

Haesoo opens the packet and squeezes the contents onto the ground. Turnip looks comical with his rump pulled all the way back and his front legs extended forward. Another round head suddenly emerges behind Turnip. Another cat with black fur—a kami. Haesoo takes out another Churu. Kami comes forward without any hesitation and gobbles up the Churu. Then the cat looks up and cries.

You want more?

Kami has no inhibitions. Compared to Turnip, Kami appears innocent and cheerful. Does being innocent and cheerful help or hurt this little creature living on the streets? Are these two cats friends, family, or is there no relation at all?

Waving off these inane thoughts, Haesoo takes out another Churu. Kami devours it again. Turnip hangs a few steps back, keeping his eyes on the two of them as if to say, One dubious move, and I'll strike. He will not allow the smallest mistake.

Kami comes toward Haesoo with a small, pink tongue poking out. Kami gets so close Haesoo could almost touch her. All of a sudden, Turnip jumps in front of Kami. This is clearly a protective gesture. Or perhaps that's just her imagination. Turnip chides Kami with a few meows, then disappears over

17

the wall. Kami looks back at Haesoo once more, then follows Turnip.

Haesoo has lived in this neighborhood for three years.

In a few more, this area will become a pretty block of nice houses. It's mostly old houses now, but on the next block over, many of the houses have been remodeled. You'll see. This block will follow soon.

Three years ago, when she visited this neighborhood for the first time, this is what the realtor had said to her. He was a middle-aged man with a decent first impression. His office was tidy compared to the worn-down exterior, every leaf of the potted plants gleamed with life. The man spoke in a gentle tone with the woman who appeared to be his wife, and they sat in comfortable silence as they gave Haesoo time to think.

Haesoo remembers all of it. She hasn't been able to throw away the business card for Purun Real Estate, either. She hasn't been able to throw away a lot of things.

Taeju was with her at the time. He was thought of as not good enough for her in many ways, yet was perhaps the perfect spouse for her. She and Taeju looked around the neighborhood together and chose this house in the end. It was a one-story house, old but solid, and the simple layout was promising for remodeling plans. Above all, it was the spacious yard that won them over.

Haesoo and Taeju planned to build a new house and turn the neglected yard into a decent garden. Tear down the wall around the property, plant grass, build a garage in one corner, and install cute little path lights. They were going to design their own wooden gate that came up to their waist. They would build a terrace on the roof. When it came to the house, there was nothing they hadn't thought of.

They were confident they could transform this old house and forsaken yard. They had the means, and they had the energy. So why is her house still the way it was three years ago? Is it because she kept pushing off the construction with work as her excuse? Is it because she didn't actually believe they could start construction any time if they wanted to? Did she truly not see the tragedy coming?

What Haesoo cannot part with is the future she might have had with Taeju. But the future she had imagined—was Taeju really part of it? Perhaps Taeju had become such a familiar, constant presence in her life that she'd neglected him. Perhaps she only thought of Taeju as a beneficiary. The inheritor of the plentiful future she had cultivated in her mind.

Haesoo picks up a pen and starts scribbling. Dizzying loops and spikes materialize on the white letter stock. None of it is legible. Haesoo cannot bring herself to write to Taeju. It's impossible. There isn't a thing she can say to him in neat rows of letters running left to right.

When she thinks of Taeju, her memories of their time together leave her disoriented. Her relationship with him has always been a maze without an exit. And now, she cannot imagine what kind of person she might have been to Taeju. She cannot ask or confirm anymore.

A draining sense of despair—of giving up—slowly descends.

Haesoo gets ready and leaves the house. Instead of heading for the park, she walks toward the alley across the street. This is not a route she likes. Unlike the usual path that becomes wider and brighter, the alley grows narrow and dark, as though in ruins. Or maybe the only place ruins are spreading and thriving is inside her.

Haesoo looks back at her house, located at the intersection between the well-lit, spacious path and the dark, narrow one. Belonging neither here nor there, her house seems to have become the line dividing two worlds. She ambles on as memories surface. She remembers the person she was before, a version of herself who believed she could suppress certain memories and emotions. The harder she tries to shake off these thoughts, the harder they cling to her. Time is a ruthless teacher.

She picks up her pace, her eyes scanning every corner of the alley, searching for Turnip. In the distance, something darts beneath a parked car.

Haesoo peers under the car. Each time she bends down to look, blood rushes to her face and a dull pain pinches the back of her knees. Haesoo is now able to get close to Turnip without scaring him, and she has his favorite snack in her pocket, but Turnip is nowhere to be seen. Haesoo can feel the wary glances of passersby.

Farther down the street, she sees a pack of children gathered under a lamppost. A familiar face shifts in and out of view among the throng.

Large duffel bag and white sports socks. Ponytail and a bigger frame than the others. But the child who gave her the Churu seems like a different person now. The energy and enthusiasm of the girl who struck up a conversation with Haesoo are gone, replaced with uneasiness and hesitation. The children's voices gradually blend into noise.

Haesoo stays where she is and watches for a moment.

Dear Minyoung,

It's been a while. I hope you are well.

I imagine you're busy. With your sessions, your lectures, the conferences, this interview and that, I'll bet the days go by in a blink. To be honest, I'm not in the mood to say nice things to you. But don't misunderstand—I'm not about to argue every little point like I used to.

I only want to know one thing.

The comment you made at the meeting to decide on my future at the counseling center. When you raised your hand to address the room, I would be lying if I said I didn't expect you to speak in my defense. Until that moment, I thought we were close.

I'm sure you remember. During your first months at the counseling center, I stayed late to help you with your work.

I always answered your late-night texts and calls, ready to help. There was no reason for me, a therapist with ten years' experience, to be so good to a fledgling just starting out. Then there was the night I rushed out to see you at your request. There was a big commotion at the counseling center that day, and I was sure you were blaming yourself. I'm sure you remember how I consoled you until daybreak. You claimed through tears that you didn't deserve to be a therapist. I'm sure you saw how I talked you up with Mr. Lee.

I didn't expect to hear what I heard from you that day. You took issue with the way I worked. You said that I was short with clients, that these complaints had been building up for years. I didn't know if it was true or not, and your comments were off-topic, but I listened. If what you were saying was true, if there were such complaints, I wanted to fix it.

As you may well remember, the mood at the meeting that day was fine enough. I would go so far as to say that I felt everyone was trying to hold on to their good opinion of me. Minyoung, you asked me: Do you really, truly regret your actions? With all your heart? I asked you what you meant. I had to. Were you asking about my conduct at work, or the incident I was embroiled in? I didn't know.

If you were asking about the incident, you should know that it had nothing to do with you. If I have to be truly sorry for something, to ask forgiveness with all my heart, you aren't the one I will tell. You had no right to ask me this question. So why did you, Minyoung? Why at the meeting,

22

with the entire staff gathered, did you suddenly bring that up?

I have thought about that moment for a long time.

I want to know why, with what intention, you asked the question. I haven't found an answer. I have never been attacked like that by a coworker. Never have I

Two days pass before Haesoo sees the child again.

Were they your friends? The kids who were with you the other night by the lamppost.

I guess you could say that, she answers.

So they're not really your friends?

No. They are my friends. They used to be, anyway.

Haesoo's nightly trips to the park happen earlier in the evening now, so early that it's still light out. Perhaps the days are getting longer. The dusky light that flowed thick in the alleys has disappeared, and the darkness descends later every day.

What were you doing there? With your friends.

Haesoo turns in the direction the girl is pointing. They turn onto another alley, half a foot narrower.

Just talking, she says.

The child follows Haesoo with her eyes on the ground. In the light of day, Haesoo thinks, the child is definitely big for her age. For a girl in the fourth grade, she is much bigger than average. The child's face glistens with sweat. Each time she pulls up the duffle bag slipping off her shoulder, she huffs to catch her breath. The shoulders of her yellow T-shirt rise and fall.

Haesoo takes smaller strides to let the child catch up and changes the subject.

She tells the girl that Turnip ate the Churu she gave her a few days ago. Haesoo says that Turnip ate the Churu out of her hand, not off a piece of paper or a leaf.

He did? Really?

Light quickly replaces the gloom on the child's face. Her prickly mood turns into curiosity in an instant.

Isn't that amazing? Haesoo casually lies. She had seen Turnip, that much is true. She'd waved the Churu packet, but Turnip didn't come near her. He patiently watched her from a safe distance. As if to say he would not give in to hunger. That he didn't need anyone's pity.

You're stubborn, aren't you?

Only when she'd squeezed the Churu on the ground and backed up quite a distance did Turnip relent and lick the Churu a little at a time. He kept his eyes on Haesoo to make it clear that she should stay back. This stirred something in Haesoo. The cat's behavior almost seemed like a parable about choosing the more difficult of two opposed needs: hunger and dignity.

Then Turnip abandoned the Churu and dashed away. Someone had spooked him by stomping their feet. When Haesoo turned around, she found a woman in a red sweater.

Don't give them anything, the woman all but shouted at Haesoo. You feed them once, they keep coming back.

Haesoo had seen the woman before. She walked her Jindo dog in the mornings and evenings. The two houses down from Haesoo's in the direction of the park were vacant, so the woman had to be living in one of two houses on the other side where tenants were always coming and going.

I don't understand it. If you feel so bad for the cats, take them home with you. What are you doing, herding all the cats in the area to this spot? It's not just the feeding. There's cat food wrappers and cans lying around, not to mention the swarms of flies in the summer. It attracts pigeons every morning, too. What's wrong with you people?

The woman had hissed at Haesoo before she went on her way. Just as Haesoo had predicted, she walked in the opposite direction of the park.

Auntie, did you really get to touch Turnip? the child asks. You didn't, did you?

I didn't get to touch him. But I think I will soon.

Really? Nah, I doubt it. He won't let you.

Haesoo and the child make their way deeper into the alley. The look of the neighborhood shifts in small increments. Past the crammed block of houses lies condo alley. Above that, homes that look like temporary structures. The hill levels off to a barren area that is not a mountaintop or a hill.

We're here.

The child runs over to a lot with a few abandoned cars. There is a small wooden crate turned onto its side. In the crate is a bowl for water and a bowl for cat food. The water bowl

25

looks muddy with leaves and dirt, and a few kernels of kibble are stuck to the bottom of the food bowl. The girl refills the food and changes the water.

Haesoo watches from a few steps back. This is a wretched place to eat. There are dried-up husks of fruit flies and swarms of ants. It's too lifeless for a place that eases hunger. An awful place to seek rest and comfort.

Is this observation also coming from a place of self-pity? Is she projecting onto street animals to feel sorry for herself?

Turnip comes all the way here to eat? Haesoo asks the girl, trying to change the direction of her thoughts.

I think so. There was another feeding spot down the hill, but it was removed because people complained. That's what the auntie said. The auntie who feeds the cats.

Haesoo looks back at the path they took. Fifteen minutes on foot for humans. She wonders how long it would take a cat.

It's not that far, I don't think, the girl says. Turnip knows a shortcut. Cats are small and quick.

The child gets up and points to a spot. A white cat is watching them in the distance. There is a tall ginkgo tree behind the cat, its leaves just starting to come in. The tree looks strong and healthy. For a moment, Haesoo is captivated by the fresh, green half-circles sprouting. The power of a tree growing from the ground. The leaves that wrestle their way out. Is she again imposing her own perspective of suffering on a common tree? She is saddened and somewhat disgusted with herself.

Hey, kitties! Are you hungry? Come and get it! Meow, meow! The girl rattles the food bowl above her head. A few more cats emerge. One of them looks like Turnip.

Isn't that Turnip over there? Haesoo asks.

The child bends down and squints ahead for a long time, then answers, It's Turnip! Yes, it's Turnip. Here, Turnip! Oh, I think he's hurt himself again. He can't even open his eyes. Do you see that, Auntie? Over there? Oh, no. What did he do this time? There, under the left eye. Do you see how red it is?

Turnip doesn't seem to be in great shape. Haesoo shields her eyes from the sun with one hand and waves at Turnip with the other. Turnip looks up at her. In the bright sunlight, Turnip and Haesoo's eyes meet.

For several days, Haesoo tries not to think about Turnip.

She tries not to recall his eyes glued together with pus, the sticky scab on his nose. The poor cat limping with one paw up. But the images only become more vivid. She does not understand why this cat is occupying her thoughts. Is she touched by this fragile living thing, or is she projecting onto the cat's suffering? Is she looking for solace in a cat in crisis? She cannot tell.

It's an endless search for meaning.

What meaning does it have for you?

That was the sentence she repeated the most when she was a therapist. When asked that question, clients would stop their outpouring of stories. They would stammer through hastily-sought answers. To Haesoo, the answers were neither accurate nor clear. Rather than pointing out that they weren't important or that they didn't carry much meaning, she would ask, And why do you think so? To help the clients realize that meaning is something one makes up.

But what meaning isn't made up? How does one tell real meaning from false?

Haesoo has long since abandoned the chase.

When she decides to help Turnip, there's no meaning behind it, nor does she want to find any. Once she makes up her mind, she sees no reason to delay.

Two days pass before she shares her decision with the child. She leaves her meet-ups with the girl entirely to chance. She never knows where or how she is going to see her, and only hopes to run into her as she walks around the neighborhood in the evening.

On Wednesday, in the late afternoon, she sees the child walking down the street with some friends. The child is trailing behind the group, carrying several colorful bags. When one of the children gestures at her, she looks up and hurries after them. Her movements seem awkward and stiff. Apprehensive.

The girl's voice does not mix with the others. When the children laugh, there is a delay before she joins them. There is a gap that isolates her from the others.

When the other children disperse left and right, the child timidly says hello, pretending she didn't see Haesoo standing there.

The two of them stand face to face in a dimly lit alley as the final light of day descends toward the ground.

Turnip? Really? You want to take him to the vet?

The child seems surprised by Haesoo's plan. She is glancing about as though anxious one of her friends might reappear. This makes Haesoo think that her friends are not friendly. They aren't welcoming of her. Haesoo casually leads the girl to a street corner and says, Yes. Wouldn't it be better to have Turnip treated soon? He didn't seem so good.

Then we have to catch him, the child says, flapping her sweat-soaked T-shirt. There's a candy bar in her hand. She turns it over but doesn't open it. She looks down at it every few seconds.

Then we'll catch Turnip. Do you know how to catch a cat?

They say you catch a cat with a trap. I'm not sure. I'll have to ask the auntie who feeds them.

Do you know how to contact her? Where can we meet her?

I don't know. I've only seen her a few times around here.

What does she look like? Can you describe her for me?

Describe her? Hmm. She's just an auntie. Regular auntie.

In Haesoo's mind, the image of an average middle-aged woman appears and fades. The child frowns intently at the candy bar in her hand and says, She has long hair. And she carries this big bag. If you ask her a question, she'll answer in a scary voice. But she's not scary. You know what I mean? At first you might think she's scary, but she's not once you get to know her.

The child can't stand it any longer. She tears open the wrapper and takes a bite of her candy bar. The chocolate leaves dark smudges around her mouth.

Haesoo takes some tissue from her pocket and hands it to her.

I don't know what she looks like. Could you help me find her? Would you like to help me?

The child nods coolly.

Are you hungry? Would you like something to eat? Your parents must be worried. You should go home first and let them know where you are. I'll come with you.

No, it's okay. I don't have to stop by the house.

The girl crams the rest of the candy bar into her mouth and puts an end to the discussion. Auntie, let's go check out the feeding place, okay?

To Mr. Hanseong Lee:

Hello.

It's Haesoo Lim. I hope this letter finds you well.

I found out through the counseling center website that the interior renovation is done. The new website seems brighter and simpler. It looks good.

I'm very sorry for all the trouble I brought to the counseling center.

That said, there is something I need to ask you. I've given a lot of thought as to the appropriateness of this question, but I can't get past it without hearing some kind of explanation from you. No matter what I do, I cannot get past it.

The question that Ms. Cho asked during our final meeting was, however you look at it, an irrelevant one. Apart from apologizing for the trouble I may have caused everyone present at the meeting, she had inappropriately demanded apology and contrition for what I had done.

The meeting that day was held officially and announced ahead of time. What I would like to know is whether her comment was also planned ahead of time, or if it was her own spontaneous decision. I would also like to know just how much weight her comment carried in deciding my future at the counseling center.

I don't have to remind you that I was terminated, and I don't know through what process this was decided. As the one who was terminated, I do not think it's too much to ask through what process you arrived at the decision. Please don't misunderstand. I'm not asking out of pettiness, and I certainly am not plotting to retaliate.

I worked as a therapist at this counseling center for over ten years. I was a founding member. You must realize what I've put into the center, how much affection and passion I held for it. If this had been just another job to me, there would be no need for me to make this request.

I do not mean to put you in a tough spot. I'm not trying to be difficult. I am trying harder than ever to understand the perspective of those who remain at the counseling center. At the same time, I'm trying to accept the fact that my career is over.

The counseling center started out with two counselors and in a decade grew into what it is now. These ten years were truly valuable to me. I do not wish for the meaning it held for me to be invalidated, so I am searching for a reason.

A specific, clear reason. The cause, the real cause of my

The search for the other auntie begins. "Waiting with no end in sight" more accurately describes the pursuit.

The child's name is Sei Hwang. She avoids the topics of school, family, and herself as though her life depends on it. Instead, she asks the questions. When there's a lull in the conversation, she seems to become anxious. Just when Haesoo is about to ask something, Sei preempts her.

Uh, Auntie. Don't you have a job? Why are you always home during the day?

Because I'm not working these days.

You don't have to work? Do you have a lot of money?

I don't have a lot, but I have enough to get by for now.

What happens when you run out of money? Can you go back to work? Can you make money again?

Of course.

What kind of work?

I was a therapist. Do you know what a therapist does?

Oh, I know. There's a therapist at my school.

Really? Then you know. Have you ever been to the school therapist?

Yes. Twice, Sei answers, and becomes quiet. Haesoo is about to ask Sei about it but Sei deflects with another question.

Auntie, where do you live?

Over there. Do you remember the red brick building we passed before?

Oh, I know. It's next door to the house with the Jindo dog. The auntie with the dog is really annoying. She's always yelling about the cats. I hate her.

Did you say you lived over there? Your parents must be worried. Wouldn't it be a good idea to stop by and let them know where you're going? Do you want to call them? Or maybe send a message?

My phone is dead anyway. It's fine. I'll just go home later. Auntie, how old are you?

How old do I look?

I don't know. Fifty? Fifty-nine? My mom is forty-two.

Forty-two? Your mom is younger than me. But that doesn't mean I'm fifty. Are you sure you don't need to tell your mother

33

where we're going? I think she'll worry. Where do you usually go after school? To study or straight home?

I go straight home unless there's dodgeball practice. You don't have to worry about my mom. It doesn't matter. Do you have a mom, Auntie? Who do you live with? Do you live with your mom?

Yes, I have a mother. I live by myself now.

Really? I really, really want to live by myself. It's great living alone, right? You eat what you want, sleep when you want, do whatever you want every single day. Right?

Haesoo derives a bit of pleasure from this. It feels nice to talk about herself with someone who knows nothing about her. Based on her answers to Sei's simple questions, Haesoo comes off as an okay person—just another person living another ordinary life.

Haesoo and Sei go around the neighborhood in a wide circle, and then once more. Sei is good at spotting the cats darting among buildings, people, and cars. Cats scurry in the alleys, neither heard nor seen. Desperate not to be seen by people. If this is learned behavior, they must have experienced something horrific and unnerving that is carved into their memories. Right and wrong, justice and injustice, good and evil—these are man-made values that do not apply to the rules of survival the cats must learn. Rules they cannot object to, that they must live by.

Haesoo finds this cruel.

What is cruel, to whom and how? Haesoo pulls herself hard out of the self-pity she is slipping into again.

Turnip does not show. The woman who feeds the cats does not show, either. Light is fading in the alleys. Haesoo checks the time and decides to send the child home. Before they part, she takes Sei to a convenience store.

Sei browses the yogurt and beverages aisle for some time, picks up and puts back the sausages, chocolates, and chips in colorful packages, then chooses a sandwich. She checks the nutritional label many times. The sandwich contains just lettuce and eggs. Haesoo gets a carton of milk, an apple, and two candy bars rung up with the sandwich.

Uh, Auntie, Sei asks as they leave the convenience store. Are you a nice person?

The child looks up at Haesoo, the plastic bag containing the milk, the sandwich, the apple, and the candy bars gently swinging.

No, I'm not a nice person.

A smile spreads across Sei's face. Haesoo's answer must be stirring the child's curiosity.

The wind gusts. It sweeps back the child's sweaty bangs, revealing a small bump of a forehead.

Sei asks, Why not? Why do you think that?

A group of people erupt with laughter as they come out of the convenience store behind them. Haesoo looks in their direction for a moment, then meets Sei's eyes again. She searches her pockets and produces a folded letter.

Because I write apology letters like this to people every day.

Sei looks down at the letter for some time, then takes it. She turns it over this way and that, but does not open it.

My dad told me not to give out my phone number to strangers. But I'll give you my number, Auntie. We have to rescue Turnip, anyway.

The child drops everything on the ground, takes a pencil from her bag, and writes her number on the folded letter.

Dear Juhyun,

How are you?

Please forgive me for dodging your calls. How is your mother? I hope she's getting better. You took such good care of me through all the rough times in my life, and yet I don't even know how you are now.

Back then, if I had done as you said, would things have turned out differently?

You were the first to let me know that there were stories going around on the internet about me. I didn't think much of it. You know how busy I was at the time. So busy I could hardly remember who I met where, and what I'd said. I didn't even remember saying those words. Even when I found out that I had said it, I didn't think it was a big deal.

It wasn't until a few days later that I learned exactly what I said. It was a comment I made on a television program. You know how these programs work. They are often scripted. Until I received my notes, I didn't even know that there was a controversy. Or the fact that this actor was the object of so many people's attention. Honestly, I didn't even know what his name was.

Juhyun, I was so worn down.

Listening to clients whose stories went around in circles, getting dolled up and saying pretentious and pointless things on television, managing Taeju's constant nagging for attention, bickering with my parents over money—I was sick of it all.

Besides, I was having the worst day. I got into an argument in the street, someone scratched my car in the bank parking lot, and I got into a screaming match with Taeju over nothing. I remember saying to myself on the way to the television studio, I wish I could just disappear. I remember wishing I could just quit everything—being a therapist, a television panelist, all of it.

I was so, so tired that day. All I could think of was how much I wanted to rest, just for one day. Where no one could find me. Back then

Haesoo walks Sei to her house and comes home. Then she opens the letter she has written and starts to read. This is a rare occurrence. She calmly follows the words and sentences that she herself chose and lined up. They are jarring to Haesoo, as if she has never seen them before.

Searing, thorny emotions emerge from a debilitating sense of defeat. These feelings gather more words. Haesoo picks up her pen and continues to write, vowing to herself that she'll mail the letter this time. That this letter absolutely will not be disposed of.

The things I said on television spread everywhere. I thought they were making a big deal out of something I said about an actor whose name and face are well known. I wasn't the only person discussing him at the time. It was ludicrous the way reporters were requesting confirmation of facts and comments from me.

At the time, everyone said that the actor had problems. That his conduct was problematic. Who would have thought that adding one more comment in support of the general consensus would cause such a big problem? How could I have known that words I don't even remember saying would grab me by the ankles and knock me down in the end?

Have you seen the memes? Me on the toilet with my arms up and mouth open? The word bubble above my head reads, "Please pay attention to me, everyone!" Each time the bubble blinks, the toilet flushing sound plays. There's another one of me opening and closing my mouth like a goldfish while dancing. The caption quotes a song, "Psycho, a little bit psycho." Fireworks pop in the background and I make a ridiculous face.

Looking at the memes, I think it's all over for me. If this is the attack I must face, what chance do I have of winning? Taking this matter seriously and discerning right from wrong using rational vocabulary will only make me seem more clownish. Fodder for more absurdity.

Who's making these memes? Who's pouring time and energy into mocking me? The people who used their keen observation to find fault in my attitude, tone, sense of propriety, character, credibility, and work ethic are articulating themselves through memes?

Juhyun, does any of this make sense to you? Can you understand why these people are so upset? Do you think I should have expected this turn of events? Should I have given in to the demands of the public that I apologize and atone? Do you think I should shut my eyes, my mouth, my ears, and do what the people want, what they expect?

Is that what you

Haesoo puts down her pen. Her hand is tingling from gripping the pen so hard. She takes a deep breath. She reins herself in as her heart races after certain words, certain sentences. Her goal is not to write a letter smudged with uncontrollable emotions. Her goal is not to write a bad letter she cannot send.

Haesoo gets dressed and leaves the house. She stands by a pile of garbage on a street corner and tears up the letter. In half, then again, she tears and tears until not a single word can be made out. As always, it has fallen far short of getting through to the recipient, not that it reveals much of an effort to do so anyway.

Haesoo is a bit of an insomniac.

She didn't sleep well before the incident, but sleeping did not require the elaborate regimen of a soldier going to battle that it does now.

Sleep. You must get some sleep, people advised her when she was in the middle of the enormous cyclone. The tragedy that began with one comment. Instead of sleeping, she read and re-read the internet comments being uploaded in real time. She searched the outpouring of anonymous comments again and again. She wandered aimlessly, following one comment after another, and lost herself every time. She learned that a few words or one line was enough to stab a person in the heart. In the days following the incident, she died hundreds, thousands of times looking at her phone and her computer screen.

And now, her dead self and her living self meet in her dreams each night. The encounter between the two occurs at the gauzy border between consciousness and dream.

Knock knock. Two people sit in the middle of a familiar counseling room. Cream-colored table and armchairs with linen covers. The view of the city outside the window is busy enough and yet quiet enough. The view of the world from this height is peaceful.

Haesoo, what worries you? the living Haesoo asks.

What people are saying about me, says the dead Haesoo.

Are you concerned about it?

Yes, I am.

What are you most concerned that people will say?

People denouncing me.

Have you heard people denouncing you? Can you tell me specifically what you heard?

Mediocre therapist screwed up so hard.

Will kill to become famous, huh? You need to get yourself a therapist first, lady.

Everyone she ever treated gotta get their money back.

Who does she think she is? Therapist destroys lives by spewing horseshit.

Who knew therapists had it so fucking easy? My dog would make a better therapist than this woman.

These are the first comments that come to mind. Words fueled by rage. But before long, specific places, establishments, and experiences are added on.

I had a session with her once, and she was really awful. Like, money's all she cares about? R Counseling Center in H District, S City. Majored in psychology at Y University. Haesoo Lim, 42. Married to Taeju Son, 43. The couple came to our restaurant sometimes. They were both unpleasant. She lives in my neighborhood. Their dog barks like crazy all night, but I haven't heard a single word of apology from her. You get the idea. Ms. Lim, remember how you treated the staff at M Café in H District like shit? Haesoo Lim, cell 010-XXXX-XXXX Taeju Son, cell 010-XXXX-XXXX.

A mix of true and false information. Locations stir the public's imagination. Numbers instill confidence. Words toss aside the gossamer cloak of hesitation and uncertainty and the indiscriminate personal attacks begin. They show no mercy.

You can't fundamentally change a person.

Physiognomy is science. Before you play therapist, take a good look at yourself in the mirror.

Your eyes are all creepy. How do you open up to a therapist who looks like that?

Wasn't she already famously bitchy?

Trash gotta take itself out. Crawl back into the hole you came from.

But there are words she fears more.

Not comments that people she has never met spit out on the internet, but words held back by the people with whom she gladly shared a life. Close friends and family whose expression and look she can read right away. The guarded look they give hides the doubt and pity that plague her. Both Haesoos, living and dead, are trapped.

Then Haesoo wakes up. And like that, she is thrown out of the world of sleep she so desperately desires. She has not once won this battle.

Two days later, on Saturday afternoon, Haesoo sees Sei's auntie near the lot where the cats' feeding station is. Haesoo is preoccupied with the ginkgo tree leaves fluttering in the wind and does not notice the woman coming toward her. It looks as if the ginkgo tree is growing bigger before her eyes. The glossy green leaves are soaking in the light and colors around them and livening up the lot.

Hey, it's Auntie! That's Auntie over there.

Only after Sei exclaims this does Haesoo turn to see the woman. The blue scarf around the woman's neck is also

42

fluttering in the wind. The woman sees Sei and waves. Sei runs over to the woman and tells her something. Haesoo stops and waits for their conversation to end.

You want to rescue Turnip? the woman comes over and asks. She is very different from what Haesoo imagined. She is younger, more chic, more energetic. Maybe it's the makeup and the suit she's wearing.

Oh, um. The house with the Jindo dog. You live down that street, don't you? I think I've seen you there a few times, right?

Haesoo, Sei, and the woman—the three of them stand awkwardly discussing this and that. The conversation begins with rescuing Turnip, the sympathy they share for the plight of the street cats, and moves on to exchanging trivial information about themselves.

Haesoo is the first to run out of things to say—about cats, about this neighborhood, about herself. She has nothing more to give. The woman tells her there are more people in this neighborhood looking out for the street cats. There's an online forum that they created, and a text group. Then she says she's been seeing lots more kittens lately. It's undeniably spring, the season of birth. What would you like me to call you? You can call me Maru Mom. I go by Maru on the online forum, though. Maru is the name of my cat.

I'm Haesoo Lim, Haesoo answers, and regrets it instantly. She didn't have to disclose her real name. But she's not used to the culture of online handles, of casually going by different names. Still, it was imprudent of her to reveal her name. She needs to be more careful, at least for now.

Auntie, are you going somewhere today? You look really pretty! Sei says, gazing at the leather keychain dangling from the woman's purse. Each time she moves, a small robot made of enamel glitters.

Really? You think I look pretty? The woman lights up. She looks at Haesoo, then at Sei, and says, I was at my friend's wedding. I came straight here without changing first. I was so worried they would be hungry because I was in such a rush I didn't get around to feeding them this morning.

Haesoo arranges to borrow a trap from the woman. She might give Haesoo some advice as well.

Before they part ways, the woman says, I just want to be sure. There are many people out there who feel bad for the cats and want to rescue them. I've seen a few of them, too. But this is not just a matter of taking the cat to the hospital. There might be more problems going on internally. We can't know ahead of time how things will play out. Are you sure you want to do this? Can you take responsibility for Turnip all the way to the end?

Responsibility. To the end. The woman wears a serious look as she says these words. Staring back at her, Haesoo wonders, Does this woman recognize me? Did she hear my name and suddenly remember who I am? Is she recalling the details of the incident as we speak? Wild speculation quickly turns into fear: at any minute, this woman is going to say things Haesoo never wants to hear.

44

Haesoo looks away from the woman and says, Yes, I can do it.

The Turnip rescue mission commences.

The next day, Haesoo waits for Sei in the alley with the trap she borrowed from Maru Mom. School's been over for some time, but Sei doesn't appear. Haesoo finds herself walking toward the elementary school.

Broad daylight. Spring sprung in the streets. A riot of scooters, bicycles, people, and cars streams past Haesoo. For the past year, she has avoided this sight, believing she would never see it again. Before the incident, she never gave these everyday pieces of life much thought.

Haesoo stands at a spot with an unobstructed view of the school gate. People glance at the large metal trap she's holding as they pass by. The children look curiously inside the trap. Haesoo waits and waits, but Sei does not appear. Looking at the schoolyard where yellow dust is blowing around, Haesoo tries to work up the nerve to go in.

After lengthy consideration, Haesoo picks up the trap and walks toward the school gate.

She has been to this school before. It was late afternoon, and she was with Taeju. They stood in a long line outside the voting station and waited for their turn. Candidates 1, 2, and 3. Change and rebuilding. Innovation and connection. She

45

was here to exercise her right to vote at a place where such slippery words were thrown around.

Haesoo does not remember who she voted for that day. Anyway, her life has changed.

Her life would have changed no matter who she voted for.

Put on a shirt with a brighter color. It looks better on you. Are you hungry? What do you want for dinner? How about the new sushi place at the intersection?

Haesoo thinks about the things she said to Taeju. She cannot remember what Taeju said in response. She can't remember what they had for dinner that evening, either. The sun-filled afternoon, the hot and heavy air, the thickening shadows of buildings. These are the hazy memories that remain.

Haesoo ambles by the monkey bars. What she is looking for, what she hopes to find—she has no idea.

She cannot remember a thing.

She tries to bring herself back to the schoolyard where the puffs of yellow dust bloom. She walks a bit faster. The sounds of children's feet and chatter drift past.

A group of children in gym clothes stand in one corner of the parking lot.

Among them, Haesoo sees a familiar face. Sei is backed up against a wall, head hanging, her arms hugging a ball. One clear voice cuts through the clamor of the children. It's a girl with a high tone and clear diction.

It's all your fault, Fatty Hwang! We're like this because you keep messing up. Don't you practice?

A patter of laughter follows.

I'm sorry. I'll practice more from now on. I'll be better next time. I can do better. It's hard to hear the mumbling voice that most certainly belongs to Sei.

How? What are you going to do next time? You said you'd do better the last time, too.

When are you going to get better?

I'm sorry.

Sorry? Can "sorry" make us win?

One kid shoves Sei in the shoulder a few times. Sei shrinks back. That's all. Haesoo watches for a while longer, then moves to a spot where she can't see them, but she can hear them.

One kid leaves, then another, then a third, and the last one, but Sei does not come out. Haesoo stares in the direction of the parking lot for a good long while before Sei comes into view, practically dragging her duffel behind her. Oblivious that her hair is concealing half her face, that her sock has rolled down to her ankle on one side, that her book bag is open. Unaware of the expression she's wearing as she walks, kicking a small rock.

The child passes Haesoo with her head down.

Sei. Sei, Haesoo calls her. The child stops and turns around. Haesoo waves hello. To her surprise, Sei's expressionless face lights up.

Dear Juhyun,

I won't be able to send this letter, but here I am writing anyway.

Lately, I've been going around with a metal trap trying to catch a cat. There's a cat I've seen around who isn't in great condition. I put food inside the trap and wait for the cat to get in. I guess "waiting out a cat" better describes what I'm doing than "catching."

Can you believe it? That I'm out doing this sort of thing?

People might see me now and think that I've fully bounced back. She's doing so well now that she's getting involved in a street cat rescue. Funny how the shameless ones always bounce back and come out on top, they might sneer. You're right. What does it matter what people think? I know it in my head, but I can't shake it off. But that's my problem.

Yesterday, I read it several times over, the letter you wrote me. The letter doesn't change, but I feel different every time I read it. Each time, I see things that I didn't see before.

I don't think I ever really thanked you. I thought there would always be another time. I've lost so many things by

I have to get out of the way, like this. When the kid on the other team throws the ball, I have to not get hit. But I got hit. So we lost. Our team lost. But I didn't get hit! The kid on the other team threw the ball, so I jumped out of the way, like this.

I didn't get hit, but the kids kept saying that I got hit, so I got off the court. The ball just flew past me. But they kept saying, I saw it. You got hit! You're out! Get off the court!

Sei ducks and gesticulates as she tries to explain what happened during the game. Haesoo nods but doesn't completely understand. She isn't entirely focused on the story, either.

We should clean up that scrape first. Do you want me to take you home? Do you want to stop by your house and then come and meet me? Haesoo asks when the child's story is over. Sei looks down at the dried blood on her skinned knee and dusts off the sand around it.

It's okay. I can go home and wash it later. I don't have to go now.

Haesoo sets the trap on the ground and bends down in front of Sei to examine the scrape. A deep abrasion has left the knee in tatters of blood, sand, and torn skin.

I think we'd better clean and put some cream on your knee first. If you don't want to go home, would you like to stop by my house instead?

The two make their way to Haesoo's house.

Haesoo opens the gate, walks across the front yard, and unlocks the door. The child follows, looking a little nervous.

Do you want to come in, or do you want to wait out here? You can do whatever feels comfortable, Haesoo says.

Sei seems unsure, but she doesn't think about it for long. She hikes up her bag and goes inside ahead of Haesoo. Haesoo follows, leaving the door open.

49

Auntie, when did you get to school earlier? Did you see me with the other kids? Sei asks, sitting on the sofa. The child's voice fills the quiet house. The silence Haesoo has long endured on her own.

You were with your friends? I didn't see them. I was going to wait for you in the alley, but you were taking so long that I came to the school to see what the holdup was, Haesoo says, beginning to clean the child's knee.

The child is clearly anxious to keep what is going on at school a secret from Haesoo, who pretends not to notice. She was a therapist, after all. An expert in human psychology. But she is well aware that the sympathy she feels for the child doesn't come from analyzing and diagnosing. The antiseptic spray foams on the scrape. Sei winces.

How did you hurt yourself? Did you fall down?

Haesoo dabs a thin layer of ointment with a cotton swab and carefully puts a bandage over it. The child's knee twitches.

Just during practice, Sei replies.

Do you have practice every day?

These days, yes. We have a competition in the fall. I have to practice harder. I'm not very good.

Does everybody have to play? I mean, is the entire school part of the dodgeball team?

No. I wasn't on the team at first. I went in as a substitute because one kid transferred to another school. Jeon Eunbin. She and I were good friends, but she transferred. So I don't get to see her anymore.

I see. You joined the dodgeball team in Eunbin's place. Did you volunteer? Because you wanted to play dodgeball? Or did someone tell you to? If it's too hard, can't you tell the team you want to quit?

Haesoo thinks the child's knee will scar. She gently wipes the sand from the scrape with a wet towel.

Nah, I like dodgeball. It's not really, really hard. It's fun. Dodgeball is fun.

That is all Sei has to say. Haesoo does not press her. She offers the child a glass of apple juice and watches as Sei gazes about the living room. Sei asks if she can tour the house. When Haesoo nods okay, the child gets up and, cautious and curious, awkward and tense, gingerly walks around the house.

What is catching the child's eye right now? Haesoo wonders. What will she discover in this house? The resentment and rage that throttle Haesoo each night? The abusive self-loathing and denial? The warscape of her inner psyche where battles erupt every day? The face of a person who's been completely and utterly flattened? Or is the child seeing something she has never paid attention to, never even noticed?

Auntie, can I go in that room?

Auntie, what's that?

Auntie, is it okay if I open this? Can I try this?

Excitement flows through the child's voice. Haesoo lets Sei do whatever she wants. The child settles at last on a crystal music box on the living room shelf.

There's this girl called Song Ha-eun. She's my friend. Was my friend in the first grade. When I went to her house, I saw something like this. Can I turn it?

Haesoo says okay. It was a souvenir she brought back from a trip she took with Taeju long ago. The child winds the music box all the way and a cheerful melody plays. The sound is so clear that Haesoo can hardly believe the tiny instrument has been neglected for so long.

Auntie, what's that? The child asks again. The child is pointing at a bronze plaque on the top shelf. The plaque is palm-sized and the words carved in relief are very small, but the child stands on tiptoe and cranes her neck to read what it says one word at a time. Wide-eyed, she looks back at Haesoo.

Wow! You received an award, Auntie?

Before Haesoo can answer, the child adds, Haesoo Lim. Haesoo Lim is your name, Auntie? The child is hopping in place to get a better look at the plaque.

Haesoo thinks back to when she received the award a few years ago. The excitement and elation she must have felt then are gone. She has nothing left to say about that day. That thing.

Auntie, Auntie. I think your name is pretty. Do you know who came up with my name? It was my mom's dad. Grandpa thought about it for a really long time and thought up my name.

Your grandfather gave you a very pretty name, Haesoo replies.

The child gives Haesoo a playful scowl and says, Grown-ups always say that when I tell them about my name. Every time. They all say the exact same thing.

But there's a grin on Sei's face that Haesoo catches.

Several days go by. Haesoo finds a strange black cat in the trap feasting on the can of cat food one day, and a flock of pigeons surrounding the trap the next. Ants and fruit flies coat the food bowl sometimes. But Turnip remains elusive.

Haesoo has come across Turnip several times since she started laying the trap. One night she saw him skulking around the trap. He circled it a few times, keeping his guard up, and quickly figured out Haesoo's intention. Then, as if to flaunt it, he stretched his upper body into the trap, took his time examining the structure inside, carefully retrieved the piece of chicken breast, and left.

Turnip's condition was growing worse. This much was clear even in the dark. The swelling around the eyes, the cut on the head that wasn't healing, the limping. All Haesoo could do was watch from a distance as this creature carried around a violent, silent pain.

And then one night, a large cat got in Turnip's way. Turnip was just leaving the trap with a treat in his mouth. They confronted each other in the narrow space between the trap and some parked cars. It began with a low growl. Their hair raised, they glowered at each other. Turnip withstood the tension without backing up. The small creature obeyed the rules of survival. He did not defy the instinctual command to stay alive.

Instead, Turnip attacked first.

A shrill cry pierced the air and fierce slashes were thrown about. Haesoo followed them as they chased each other down the street, pouncing and tumbling. Looking under the parked cars, Haesoo passed the lamp post with the piles of garbage, nearly got hit by a scooter, and reached the end of the wall.

The large cat retreated.

Turnip stood his ground until the cat was completely out of sight. Then he looked up at Haesoo and collapsed softly on his stomach. His small frame rose and fell quickly as he tried to catch his breath. His eyes shone in the dark like two fine lines of light. Haesoo could not decide if the expression she saw there was fear or relief.

Or maybe what she was seeing was life or death. Maybe neither.

One thing was clear: another crisis had been overcome. Haesoo pulled a can of salmon from her pocket and moved closer to Turnip.

I will not attack you. I will not harm you, Haesoo tried to say with her expression and body language, not words.

Turnip held his breath and watched her. The headlights of cars and scooters going by revealed snatches of Turnip's small, scrawny body. A long while later, Turnip slowly got up and came toward Haesoo. Head tilted to one side as if it hurt to chew, Turnip never took his eye off his surroundings as he ate.

Life is exhausting, isn't it? It took everything in Haesoo not to say these words out loud as she gave Turnip another helping from the can. Turnip sniffed it and tried his best to swallow. They were so close she could have reached out and touched his nose. Turnip made frequent eye contact.

A delicate bond had formed between Haesoo and this small creature. Human and animal. Two beings who cannot make full use of the power of language, who are allowed only the most limited interaction of giving and receiving food and water. Despite the adversity of a complete and mutual lack of understanding, Haesoo felt her pure intentions had finally got through to Turnip. Or maybe this was a strange belief on her part, a vain hope.

Turnip looked up at her and cried.

The sound was hardly audible, close to a sigh. So as to not seem threatening or scare him, Haesoo bowed a little, blinked, and took a few steps back. Turnip slowly lapped up the rest of the food, looked up at Haesoo again with a blank expression, and turned. Haesoo took that to mean "goodbye." A promise to meet again. She did not follow, but stayed where she was and watched the creature vanish out of sight.

Putting everything on the line. A fight that can cost you everything. A battle to protect no more than your miserable self.

What was it that Haesoo saw that night? What did Turnip show her? Or rather, what was she trying to see in Turnip?

To Mr. Seong-mok Lee:

Hello.

I'm Haesoo Lim. I'm sure you remember me.

"Killing Words: A Therapist's Comment Drives Man to Death"

I still remember the title of the article you wrote for the paper. Some memories never fade and will follow me to the grave. To be frank, I wasn't able to read the article all the way through. I tried several times, but I couldn't.

I'm sure there are parts of me that are embarrassed and ashamed. That want to avoid facing the mistake I made. But unlike what people think, that isn't all. Not all of what is said in your article—that I threw words around like a weapon and drove a person to death—is the truth.

Let me ask you this: how can you put so much speculation and intuition in an article meant to be read by so many people? How could you send it to print without asking me, the subject of the article, to confirm any of the facts?

What's done is done, and you can't undo it. It will take time, and time will reveal the truth. This was the advice people gave me in the wake of the article's publication. For some time, I tried to rely on this advice. I believed that there were things I had to endure, even if I were to take the many intricate forms of legal recourse my lawyer suggested.

I am pressing charges against you next week. You will be held legally accountable for your actions, and you will be examined in a court of law. I am sure you know that after your article came out, others with similar stories also cropped up. I will hold you responsible for that as well.

If you have something to say in response

On the way home, after checking again on the trap, Haesoo sees a group of people standing in front of the convenience store.

Half a dozen people surround a woman seated on a bench. The woman is still, her head bowed. It looks like she's crying.

People are awful. You must be in shock. God, I can't even imagine . . . It's okay. Take a deep breath. We've got to stay strong. Especially through stuff like this, says a woman.

It's the house with the Jindo dog, right? Or the barbecue place over there? No, it must be the mean old man on this street. The one who hoards metal? Do you think it's him?

Another voice joins in, then another, until the voices turn into a din. At last, Haesoo recognizes the woman on the bench as Maru Mom—the woman who goes to the ginkgo tree lot every day to feed the cats, who lent her the trap and offered her tips. Haesoo stands still, unable to decide if she should say hello or just walk by.

Maru Mom sees her and jumps up from the bench.

Oh, hello. I was wondering how you were. How's Turnip? Did you rescue him?

Maru Mom is calmer than she was last time. She wipes her tears with both hands and seems tired as well.

Not yet. I've been leaving the trap at the same place every day, but he won't go in.

The group's eyes are on Haesoo. She forces herself to resist the impulse to turn around and walk away.

Oh, you're the one who's rescuing the ginger cat, one of them says. Maru Mom told us about you. He's neutered, isn't he? He won't go in the trap because he's been trapped before. These cats are so clever.

The ginger cat on this street? Isn't he still a baby? He can't have been neutered already.

People are talking to her. Talking at her. She can't get a word out. Her mind goes blank. She has forgotten how to talk to people.

A memory comes to mind: the manager of a Chinese restaurant she and Taeju used to frequent. One day, when she was at the counter paying for a meal, he said to her, Would you be very offended if I asked you not to come to our restaurant for a while?

At first, Haesoo didn't understand what he meant. He knew the couple well enough to ask after them and make little jokes. She thought maybe they were redecorating the restaurant or taking a long break. Taeju, who was standing behind her, was the one who picked it up.

Don't come to your restaurant? What do you mean? he snapped. Don't come back from now on?

The manager looked over at the patrons in the hall and said quietly, Some of our customers take pictures and post them on social media. We try to stop them, but we can't get them all. If a picture of you eating at our restaurant gets out, it could put us in a difficult position.

For three years, she had eaten at that restaurant three or four times a month, sometimes had company dinners there, and warmly asked after him every time. She did not demand to know whether he had forgotten about it. Instead, she squeezed Taeju's hand so he would not say what she was thinking.

Okay. Thank you for your honesty, Haesoo said. She meant it. She signed the receipt and took back her credit card. She was so tired of people that she could now say these things out loud. Tired of being among people who pretended everything was fine, in the painfully mannered way they had of spinning out endless interpretations and subtexts of the things that were said.

If they had just reviled her, condemned her, given her disgusted, loathsome looks that she cannot unsee, if they had done that instead, she would have writhed and raged and put her agony on full display like the protagonist of every tragic plot. She would have given them what they wanted.

People must know. That this façade of politeness and decorum, these oblique gestures excruciate her the most. That this is the safest, most potent punishment they can deliver.

By the time the restaurant kicked her out, she had already forgotten how to talk to another person. Or perhaps, as Taeju said, she was using silence as a weapon to refuse all communication. Images of Taeju consoling, persuading, nagging, and chiding her to open up surface and fade.

Was he neutered? I don't think I had a good look because he's still a baby. By the way, where did you set up the trap? He won't go in unless he's hungry, but he may not be that hungry because there are feeding stations everywhere. But if we stop putting out food, the other cats will starve. It's a problem.

A look emerges on Maru Mom's face. The plucky, strong person Haesoo saw before returns.

Haesoo keeps her eyes on the ground and says little. Tufts of green grass have sprouted between the sidewalk bricks. She is disgusted at herself for trying to find even the tiniest trace of suffering in everything around her. She is disgusted that she finds comfort in it.

Does he let you touch him? He doesn't, right? They're harder to deal with after the rescue. You can't release a sick cat back into the street. You wouldn't be willing to take him in, would you, somebody asks Haesoo.

I haven't thought about it, she replies.

Then Maru Mom tells Haesoo about the cat that got sick after eating something. Someone poisoned it on purpose, she says, her face saddening again. Someone adds that a bunch of kittens turned up dead last summer and fall. Another says that horrific testimonies about street cats come up on the internet all the time, and yet another complains that the police investigations are cursory and never yield any results.

Haesoo doesn't respond. The women who were trying to read her seem to withdraw their attempt to gain her empathy, to get Haesoo on their side. A heavy silence descends.

This one hardly made it one year. Look at it. It's about the size of Turnip, wouldn't you say?

Maru Mom points down at the cat kennel by the bench. In the rectangular kennel lies a limp, white thing. It's a small, scrawny cat. It looks like a crumpled sheet of newspaper.

Is it dead? Haesoo asks, thinking she's an idiot for asking.

Yes. We found it too late. People are so vicious, don't you think? What did the cats ever do to deserve rat poison? We could have taken it to the vet if we'd found it sooner. People are just so, so horrible.

Haesoo freezes at the sight of the lifeless cat. She's become numb to feelings like sadness and anger.

What's going to happen to it now? Haesoo asks, almost to herself.

We're taking it to the funeral parlor tomorrow to be cremated and say our goodbyes.

Cremated? There are funerals for animals?

Haesoo realizes that she doesn't know anything about this. After a long pause, she manages to pick one question out of the dozens of stupid questions that occur to her: Does this happen a lot?

She is thinking of Turnip.

Dear Taeju,

I found your diary in the storage room a few days ago.

Diaries written in pencil when you were a boy, that your mother bound together into one volume. I didn't know it was in there. I know you told me to just get rid of all of your stuff, but I thought I should save this. It's memories of your childhood that have nothing to do with me. Records of your life you wrote with your own hands when you were very young. If you want, I can mail it to you.

One more thing. Your college diploma, your letter of appointment, and your certificates are here. You can always get a new one issued, but these are the originals. What do you want me to do with them? I don't know if it's appropriate for me to write to you about them, but I thought I would ask because they matter to you.

The tabletop you chose and hand-polished is still in the storage room as well. The toolbox and the metal stand, too. Yesterday, I found two of your favorite geodes in the yard. The one with the pale pink highlights and the wave pattern one. You said they were a gift from someone's trip abroad. Or did you buy them yourself? I don't remember, to be honest. I can mail you these as well.

The pictures and painting you liked and your vinyls are packed in a separate box. I put them away one day to get them out of my sight and forgot about them. I can mail them, too. I'm sure I'll find more things I need to send you. Clothes. Shoes.

Every time I get a chance, I

A few days later, Haesoo runs into Maru Mom again. She is again standing in the center of a quarrel, two large women and an old man on either side of her.

Hey, who the hell are you?

Maru Mom is near the spot where Haesoo leaves the trap every night to catch Turnip—the trap that clever Turnip will never, ever get caught in. Haesoo thinks this is all pointless. She needs a new strategy for catching Turnip. But she has no alternatives at the moment.

Like I said, there's a sick cat that needs to be rescued. Someone has to get it fixed.

A sick cat's none of my business. Why do you keep leaving food here? That's what I'm asking. Why are you rounding up all the neighborhood cats to this very spot?

Sir, the cats were always here. They live here because they were born here. I didn't round them up.

Look at all the food in the cage there. Animals come looking for food. You lure the cats by leaving food there. Get it?

Sir, that's just a trap. It's meant to trap a sick cat.

Hey, I don't care what it's for. Just get it out of here. Put it in front of your house. How many times do I have to tell you? This has got to stop.

You don't live here, either. This is the street. It's for everyone to use.

63

Maru Mom doesn't back down. The others don't, either. They have taken a firm position based on their own rationale. Haesoo does not judge who is right or wrong.

She fights the urge to choose a side. In a way, taking a clear position is easier than not taking one. It's a quick, tempting way of identifying who you are. When it's not personal, anyone can take a side on a matter and withdraw their support just as quickly.

But Haesoo has not forgotten that she threw her life into turmoil for making the same mistake.

I don't get it. Why are you in someone else's neighborhood causing trouble? Sure, you like animals. That's your right. But why do the people in some other neighborhood have to suffer because of you? What do you have to say to that?

What suffering?

Are you deaf? Have you even been listening to me? Is anything getting through in there?

The voices grow louder. Haesoo steps into the middle of the quarrel and says, I left this trap here. It wasn't her. I'll remove it as soon as the cat is caught.

People turn to look at Haesoo. She recognizes a few familiar faces. People she must have passed by on the street. People who know about her house, family, and work. People who have a good grasp on the chasm between her former life and her current one.

I'll leave it out for a moment just at night and put it away early in the morning. I'm sorry, Haesoo adds. As respectfully as possible and using polite body language, she tries to appease them.

It's just a few hours every day. You have nothing to worry about.

The people continue to look irritated but have nothing more to add. As if to say this was the groveling they were looking for. As if to remind her that their consent is mandatory. Or perhaps they just feel sorry for Haesoo, like everyone does.

You're the lady who lives in the house over there, right? We're going straight to you if there's a problem.

The crowd disperses, grumbling to themselves. Maru Mom glares at them without a word.

Haesoo gathers up the things scattered on the ground that clearly belong to Maru Mom.

I don't understand these people. Why are they bullying me about something that has nothing to do with them?

They'll leave you alone for now.

No, they won't. They'll get even worse. They have one more person to bully now, so they'll alternate and pick on both of us. There's no solution with these people.

Haesoo fights the urge to tell Maru Mom that she's all bullied out. That enduring endless lashings of hostility and hate builds tolerance.

It must be difficult for you, the constant conflict with people. Listening to their complaints.

Listening to complaints? Arguing? That doesn't matter. What difference does it make when the cats' lives are at stake?

I'm not going to sit around and watch them die. Every time I turn a corner, I see one and then another. How can I pretend not to see?

Anger seeps into Maru Mom's voice. Haesoo notices red scratch marks on Maru Mom's arms. The streetlight around the corner blinks. Maru Mom looks at it and says, I would be lying if I said this isn't difficult. Looking after the cats is tough enough as it is without these people ganging up on me. I am unwelcome and picked on everywhere I go, and I don't enjoy that. No one would. I keep telling myself that I'm going to quit, that I'm really going to quit this time, but quitting is hard, too. I can't let the cats starve because I can't handle being picked on. That's not right.

Maru Mom's eyes meet Haesoo's, seeking support. Haesoo nods. Maru Mom is right in that the street belongs to no one. If the street is for everyone, the rights of other living things like cats and pigeons would be included. All living things that come into the world have a life they must live out. This is not a matter of choice.

Haesoo understands this.

Haesoo packs a growing list of things before leaving the house.

Trap and kibble, smoked chicken breast and Churu, catnip in both powder and spray form, garbage bag, clear plastic gloves. On some days, she also packs a wide-brim hat and a gallon of water, an umbrella and waterproof tarp, hand wipes and a spool of plastic twine, things she cannot transport without a plastic cart. Haesoo sometimes worries that people will see her walking around with a metal trap and a plastic cart and think of her as a crazy cat lady.

Before it happened—if the incident hadn't happened—Haesoo would never have taken on something like this. She would have held on to the belief that she could distinguish between things she can and cannot do, must and must not do. She would have believed in the line—then firm—between things that do and do not require her attention. Now, Haesoo can't be sure of anything. In some way, she has accepted the fact that the master of her life isn't her, but life itself. Avoiding the eyes of the neighbors, she waits with the trap for Turnip at the ginkgo tree lot during the day. When Turnip makes the occasional appearance, he is always in bad shape and showing no signs of getting better.

One afternoon, Haesoo sees Turnip and Kami eating kibble together. It's raining. Shielding herself with a black umbrella, Haesoo squats in a corner and watches them. Raindrops fall and little grains of sand bounce up. Each time a gust of wind sweeps through the lot, the ginkgo leaves lean to one side and intensify the sound of rain.

Kami does not leave after her fill of kibble. She stays by Turnip's side as he swallows the kibble one kernel at a time. Kami licks around Turnip's eye and grooms his matted fur with her tongue. She seems to be cheering him on to take one more bite, just one more.

67

Haesoo tries moving the trap covered in a plastic tarp from one side of the lot to another. But the cats ignore the trap. This strategy is not going to work.

Hello.

Haesoo waves. Kami comes over, followed cautiously by Turnip. Kami shakes the rain off her body. Droplets fly in all directions and soak Haesoo's cheek and chin. Turnip doesn't seem to have the strength to shake off the water. He stands off a bit in the rain as if to say, What choice do I have? A string of drool hangs from Turnip's mouth, threatening to fall at any moment. Brief glimpses of his canines show red, swollen gums, and the front paw that Turnip doesn't put weight on looks flattened.

It's apparent that Turnip is in pain. Pain and suffering has seized this frail creature.

Turnip, come here. Come here.

Haesoo extends her hand to Turnip. Kami approaches. Trusting and childlike, Kami rubs her nose on the tip of Haesoo's finger. Then she gently taps Haesoo on the hand with her paw. The rain soaks Kami as she romps. Haesoo wiggles her fingers and plays with Kami. But her eyes are on Turnip.

Her heart is breaking.

Pity, sympathy. The usual things people feel when they see a poor, defenseless animal. Haesoo does not know what she is feeling. She isn't sure if she pities the pain that Turnip is in right now, the life that exposes Turnip to such pain, the time Turnip has suffered through so far, or the suffering to come that may last for who knows how much longer.

If she really feels sorry for Turnip, or only for herself. Maybe both.

Next day, Haesoo goes to see Maru Mom.

When she gets to the milk distribution center with the closed shutter as per Maru Mom's instruction, she sees Maru Mom walking over far down the street; she is wearing a loose-fitting dress and looks tired, as if she has just woken up. Maru Mom is carrying a yellow drop trap and a pair of thick gloves that come up to the elbows.

You know what's important? Not quitting. Most people try it a few times and give up if it doesn't work. They say it's just not going to happen. I don't think that way. If you don't give up, you'll catch the cat eventually.

Maru Mom seems to want Haesoo to find even the tiniest hint of hope in her words.

Is that right? Haesoo mumbles, looking down at the yellow drop trap.

Maru Mom tells Haesoo about the things she's learned in the seven years she's been taking care of street cats. How it's changed her life, how merciless people out there can be, and the traps, schemes, and ruckus she was pulled into.

That must have been hard, Haesoo says. Didn't you feel like giving up sometimes? I mean, I wonder if there were times when you felt like quitting altogether.

69

Maru Mom replies, That phase is over for me. I don't think that way anymore. It doesn't help at all.

Maru Mom points at the drop trap on the ground and asks, Guess how many sick cats I rescued with this thing?

Haesoo does not answer, and Maru Mom promises to give her the exact number if Haesoo succeeds in safely rescuing Turnip. She's trying hard to pump her with motivation, or something like it.

Haesoo wants to know why Maru Mom keeps doing this despite everything. Why witness the miserable lives of street cats that don't improve or change from one day to the next? What does she learn from sticking with it?

Reason? There's no reason. Cats don't live for a purpose. They just do. Same goes for me, Maru Mom answers, and turns to go as if to scold Haesoo for constantly searching for meaning. She reminds Haesoo to get in touch with her if she needs help.

To Ms. Hanna Ju:

I hope this letter finds you well.

I was told that you called the counseling center a few times looking for me. As you may have heard, I am taking a break from work at this time. I am unable to let you know when I will be returning to the counseling center or going back to work. If you want, I can ask the counseling center to refer you to a therapist who will be able to help you. I can send your files to the next therapist. If you don't feel comfortable with that, I can also ask the counseling center to dispose of your files according to protocol.

I am very sorry we had to stop sessions so abruptly.

I don't know if my saying so will help, but I believe you will get through this period in your life. As I have always said, I never doubted the strength of all the good things in your life. Even if you don't see them all now. Always remember that you are stronger and more beautiful than you think.

I sometimes recall the question you asked during our first session. It was more of a demand than a question: *Don't try to comfort me. Give me a diagnosis. I don't need to be consoled. I need a solution.* Seeing your gradual transformation each week was a great surprise and delight to me.

If there is anything I can do to help you, please feel free to let me know. Through our times together, I was also able to

Where are you? Are you at home?

Sometime before noon, Haesoo gets a call from her mother. She lets the phone ring a few times before answering. Her mother is one of the few people who don't demand an answer from her. She is happy just to have Haesoo listen.

Your father and I went to the baker's funeral last week. Remember the bakery at the market? Hosandang Bakery?

Yeonu, who you used to play with when you were little, she's got three kids already. Grabbed my hand and wept, saying she never imagined her father would pass away so soon. Just when she thought she could finally give him something back. She's been a softie since she was a little girl. She told me it was a heart attack. He was such a hardworking man. And he died so suddenly.

Haesoo sits on her stoop and listens to her mother. The dry, barren yard of winter is giving way to green nests of grass. The ripening warmth of spring is filtering into her yard.

By the way, I saw on the news yesterday that fish is bad for you. Big fish, even mackerel, are the worst. Don't you like mackerel? Stay away from mackerel for now. There's other seafood you can eat. Are you listening to me? What are you feeding yourself these days? You start skipping meals and snacking and telling yourself, Oh, it's just one meal—that's how you make yourself sick. And once you lose your health, you lose everything. You have got to feed yourself, even if it's just you. Yes, it's a lot of work for one, but you've got to feed yourself. Are you listening to me?

Yeah, I'm here.

Outside the gate, her neighbor walks down the street with her Jindo dog. A delivery man rolls a tower of boxes into the side street. A scooter sails by, blasting music.

So, are you coming for a visit?

Yes. I'll visit soon, Haesoo reassures her mother, telling her what she wants to hear. This is a way of saying what cannot be said and hearing what cannot be heard. Playing "find the hidden picture." Haesoo searches her mother's words for things she isn't saying, and her mother searches Haesoo's silence for things she cannot say. They have learned over time to hear the words left unsaid. They now know that this is the only way to avoid hurting each other.

When articles about Haesoo began pouring out, her mother called and asked, Haesoo, is something going on with you?

At the time, Haesoo was unable to take in even the most harmless comment from anyone. She was filled to the brim with comments. One more would break the surface tension and cause an overflow. The emergency button would light up, the alarm would flash, the siren would blare, and Haesoo would lose all control.

It's just a problem at work.

What problem? Is it serious? Your father tried to call you so many times, but I stopped him. He doesn't know that I'm calling you now. I'm worried about you. Do you have someone you can reach out to for help? What does Taeju think?

I'm taking care of it. Don't worry, Mom.

Haesoo, people got it wrong, didn't they? Isn't it a misunderstanding? Aren't they accusing you of saying something you didn't say? God. Is it true that this man died? Did he really kill himself? I don't know. I can't make heads or tails of it.

Her mother's words were like kindling—Haesoo's anxiety roared into a blazing fire once again. A frightening blaze of fire. A frightening amount of water. Things she could not handle possessed her in an instant.

Don't read the articles, Mom. Don't go online. Don't do anything.

Stop. You can't make this go away by closing your eyes. You should do something. If the person is dead, you can't win. You can't fight a dead person and win.

Haesoo felt attacked by her mother's words. As though her mother was accusing her of saying the things she said on television out of anger, with malice. Her mother was blaming her.

Haesoo, everyone makes mistakes. Did I ever tell you this story? What your grandmother went through when you were very young? At first, we didn't think much of it. It really wasn't a big deal at first. One day, your grandfather—

Mom, Haesoo interrupted her mother. Mom, anyone could have said it. Many other people besides me, in fact, did say it. How could I have known that this would get so blown out of proportion? What do I have to do? Tell them I meant to say what I said? That I intended to make him do what he did? That it's all my fault? You think I asked for this to happen? You think I killed him? He killed himself. He took his own life.

With that, Haesoo silenced her mother.

Now, Haesoo cannot read any judgment in her mother's voice. Her mother does not bring up that subject anymore. But it isn't avoidance. She isn't trying to judge Haesoo through silence. Her silence doesn't contain hidden intentions or messages. Has her stance changed? Has she noticed that the lines Haesoo drew between mistake and wrongdoing, innocent and framed, are beginning to blur?

Haesoo, go out for long walks when it's sunny out. See things and listen to things, whatever they are. It's foolish to hate the world.

Haesoo tells her that she will, and hangs up. Then she gets dressed, as if to show that she has made up her mind, and leaves the house.

A group of children stand to one side of the schoolyard.

The children flock from one side to the other, then stand in a row. The dodgeball game is about to start. They quickly jump and duck out of the way of the flying ball. The dark-haired heads gather and scatter. They cheer each time the ball is tossed high in the air.

Haesoo's gaze stays on the energy and life bursting out of the children.

From a distance, it's a peaceful moment in the afternoon. But the game must begin. The children gather.

They stand along the back and sidelines, so close they're shoulder to shoulder. One child steps into the court. Bigger frame than her peers, mincing steps, occasional head tilt to the left—it's Sei.

Sei is the only one standing inside the attack zone.

Begin! someone cries. With that, the children pass the white ball. It is quickly tossed from one kid to another outside the lines. The ball flies past Sei, to her left, then her right, and back, as she stands in the center of the attack zone. To Haesoo, Sei looks stiff, awkward, and frightened. What are these children doing? Is this a training exercise they invented? Instinctively, Haesoo knows that it isn't.

Suddenly, the ball is whipped into the center.

Hey, Hwang Sei, someone shouts. Get out of the way! Duck! Keep your eyes on the ball.

You're out. What are you, a moron?

The ball is passed around the players in the attack zone again and picks up speed. A strange rhythm begins to take shape. The rhythm raises the tension and stokes fear. Haesoo realizes that this is no different from hunting—cornering prey, driving terror and dread.

But that isn't the most striking thing.

Sei seems helpless from where Haesoo stands, but the child concentrates rather than panicking or surrendering to this situation. Sei's movements pick up speed. She doesn't take her eyes off the ball and throws herself out of the way when it comes at her. She ducks, jumps, twists, and touches the ground. She trips several times but does not give up.

Sei is fast, and so is the ball. Both of them are unyielding.

Fatty Hwang! Get moving! You snoozing?

The ball strikes Sei on the shoulder and flies up.

Catch the ball! Hey! Catch it!

The ball strikes Sei on the thigh and bounces off.

Hey! Keep your eyes open! How can you see the ball if you close your eyes? Hey, open those eyes!

The ball strikes Sei's head, hand, back, and foot. The ball stalks her relentlessly and charges at her without rest.

No one would call this a fair game. This clearly goes against the spirit of sportsmanship. But Haesoo does not act imprudently. Wearing the authoritative face of an adult, barging into the children's world, lecturing on right and wrong and ordering them to play nice isn't a good solution. It only exacerbates the problem. The voice of one oblivious outsider isn't going to change anything.

Uh, Auntie. Did you see me play dodgeball? Sei asks after all the other children have gone. She looks tired and mortified.

Haesoo looks down at the yellow drop trap she put on the ground and says, Just a little. I borrowed this from Maru Mom yesterday. Let's try the rescue with this today.

Sei sits down on the steps, takes off her sneakers, and shakes the rocks out of them. Her gestures are gruff and surly.

If you want to say something, you can say it, Haesoo says.

Auntie, don't come to school to meet me from now on. It would be better if we meet at the empty lot instead. Where the cats eat.

Okay.

The thick, heavy afternoon light follows them as they cross the schoolyard to the gate. When they reach the gate, with effort, Haesoo abandons the idea that she can comfort Sei with words, with language. She understands that the strong belief she held as a therapist was, in truth, brittle. She cannot be sure of anything she says. She cannot predict how words will be twisted and misconstrued. Perhaps that was the essence of communication she should have learned sooner.

Are you hungry? Haesoo asks. Should we get a bite to eat before we go? Do you want a soda?

Sei swings her tote bag this way and that, but does not answer.

Haesoo tries again. I'm sorry I came to your school. I will wait for you in the lot from now on. I won't come to your school.

Sei gives her a look and says, Keep your promise. No take-backs.

To Mr. Kyungjin Choi

Hello.

I'm sorry for taking so long to get back to you on my thoughts regarding the suit against the reporter Seong-mok Lee. To be honest, I keep changing my mind. I don't know what's holding me back, but then I wonder if I really have to pursue this. I'm not sure which of the issues concerns me more.

I've been thinking about what you said last time we met: what's done is done. Try to resolve the problem. Find a solution. Take responsibility for your mistakes, but seek apology and compensation for the injury you suffered. The two are separate matters independent of each other. Don't overthink it. If you wait, your window of opportunity will slip away.

I have decided to press charges against Seong-mok Lee and

the people who posted libelous comments online. I understand that this could make life harder for me. Getting an apology and recompense isn't going to solve everything. But, as you said, I'm telling myself that certain matters do call for action.

Please let me know via email the specifics as to how you intend to proceed. I am curious about what others have decided to do. Are you also taking on Mr. Seung-pyo Lee and Ms. Sujin Jang's cases?

And one more thing, what I meant to bring up before

It occurs to Haesoo that patiently waiting for Turnip each day isn't the best strategy. She needs a more proactive, creative approach.

On Saturday afternoon, she and Sei go out to the ginkgo tree lot together. It's a beautiful day. The forsythias lining the walls have gone, the dazzling cherry blossoms have scattered, and the crimson-tinted rosebuds are waiting to bloom. Once the roses fall, it will officially be summer.

Auntie, if we rescue Turnip today, are you going to take him to the vet? Vets are very expensive. It's because animals don't have insurance. That's what my dad told me.

Yes, I imagine it is. I should ask Maru Mom if she could recommend a vet. I haven't thought about that at all. Have you ever been to a vet, Sei?

Yes. Just once.

When?

When Bingo got sick. Bingo was my grandma's dog. He was a white Jindo dog.

Bingo must have been very sick. Is he better now?

No. He's dead.

Rather than asking questions, Haesoo waits for Sei to speak.

My grandma also died at the hospital. Do you think the vet will fix up Turnip if we take him? Do you think he'll get better? He won't die, will he?

The child has a surprising way of thinking. Sometimes it races far ahead of Haesoo's.

The hospital is the place to go to get fixed up when you're sick, Haesoo answers. And sometimes things don't work out. If it's too late or if the patient is too sick, there's nothing the hospital can do. But Turnip will be fine. Don't worry.

Sei purses her lips like she wants to say something, but doesn't. The effort casts a light veil of shadow on her face. The yellow drop trap, bag of snacks, metal trap, and huge catching net—the list of things they have to carry gets longer and slows them down.

Is that heavy? Give me that. I'll take it.

It's okay. I'm very strong. Look!

Sei walks ahead of Haesoo to prove her point. When they arrive at the ginkgo tree lot, they're both dripping with sweat. They put down their things and look around for a good spot, a place along Turnip's path that could throw off the clever, vigilant cat.

Haesoo places the metal trap a few feet from the ginkgo tree, and the yellow drop trap a few feet from the metal trap. She lifts one end of the drop trap off the ground and props it up with a wooden stick. Unlike the metal trap that doesn't close until the animal is all the way inside, the drop trap doesn't have a bottom. It's easier to lure the cats in. The texture of the floor is key here. Cats with bad eyesight have to depend on other senses.

Sei, do you want to try pulling the string?

Sei pulls the string attached to the wooden stick, making the drop trap fall. Haesoo carefully chooses the position of the wooden stick, lifts the drop trap as high as possible, and asks Sei to test it again. Then she places a few juicy pieces of chicken breast and settles down far away from the trap.

Do you think Turnip will come? Haesoo asks. Do you think we'll get him today?

Sei answers halfheartedly, then takes out her phone and stops responding altogether.

Haesoo looks up at the ginkgo tree growing more lush by the day and talks about something else.

She talks about the mistakes she makes every night knowing she'll regret it when day breaks. She talks about the loneliness that pulls her into the current and crushes her resolve.

Sei, I called a friend last night. But she told me not to call her for the time being. I think she doesn't want to talk to me.

Your friend, Auntie? Your friend told you not to call? Why not?

We got into a fight once. I think she's still upset.

81

When did you fight? What did you fight about?

Haesoo can't explain it in terms of small conflicts that arise when children play, like wanting a turn first, taking more than one's share, exchanging hurtful words, or shoving. Simple jealousy, competition, or misunderstanding. The conflict between Haesoo and Juhyun isn't anything like that. If the reason were that simple, the conflict would not have persisted for so long. This was a matter of difference in worldview and philosophy, hard to reconcile.

Haesoo, you don't have to defend yourself to me—this was the advice Juhyun gave when the incident first occurred. I don't need an apology. This is not something that happened between the two of us. It might help you to talk to me about it. But this isn't the way to go. This is not a solution. You must meet these people. The family of that man. Whoever it is. If you don't, this is never going to go away. I'm not saying you should do this for their sake. Do it for your own sake.

But Haesoo could not meet with those people. Those people, the family of the man who committed suicide a few months after she made that controversial comment about him on television. They did not want to meet with her. Actually, phrasing it that way is misleading. Haesoo never requested a meeting with them, so she doesn't know if they wanted to see her or not. To them, Haesoo was just one of many deplorable people who made flippant, rude, ignorant comments.

Haesoo could not meet with them. She had and still has nothing to say to them.

Not long after the incident, however, Juhyun brought her to meet the man's mother. Juhyun pulled up in front of a three-story community center. Each time the large double doors opened, old people in colorful jackets emerged in groups.

Do you know where we are? Juhyun asked, adjusting the volume on the radio. Haesoo did not answer. She had an inkling of what was happening.

In the distance, an old lady with a cane and floral print bag was slowly making her way down the steps. She kept her eyes on her toes even as she said hello to those around her and chatted with them. There was another old lady squatting by the entrance who was rummaging through her bag. Each time the wind blew, the blue scarf around her neck billowed as if about to fall off. Another old lady, then another, kept appearing in the distance.

Jeonggi Park's mother is here. Do you want to go inside?

Long before Juhyun said those words, Haesoo's eyes were already searching for her. Meet her and then what? What do you want me to do? Haesoo refrained from asking the questions out loud and quietly watched the old ladies go by. Slow steps, gray hair, gaze that fell to the ground like a scale beam pulled down by weights.

Haesoo was somewhat shocked.

It wasn't the rush of thoughts on what one must and must not do, or can and cannot do, but the fact that she had never pictured a flesh-and-blood person on the other end of this tortuous train of thought. Victim and family, truth and conjecture, plea and rebuttal. Beyond these words was a breathing, walking, talking person living a life that had been dealt to her—a person Haesoo had never imagined.

And here she was, supposedly a real person.

Haesoo knew. Knew what Juhyun wanted from her. Knew what she had to do and could do in that moment, so she rejected it all. She talked about hiring a lawyer, blamed the context and angle, and pretended to deliberate the right time and the right way instead.

Haesoo has not once regretted her decision.

Juhyun doesn't get it. She is a serious person who has always taken everything, including this matter, far too seriously. If we cannot find a middle ground, Haesoo had told herself, we will drift apart. Haesoo thought she was prepared for it—to lose a thirty-year friendship over this. She was prepared to lose the person who was probably the only witness to the joys and happiness of her childhood, who listened to her, talked Haesoo through her feelings, and relentlessly tried to pull her out of an emotional ditch. Haesoo decided she could no longer take Juhyun's advice.

Just as she had lost her acquaintances, folks she knew from school, coworkers at the counseling center. Just as her relationship with Taeju had imploded.

Haesoo thought this unsavory end was something she had to bear. Losing some treasured thing like an arm was the punishment she had to suffer.

So why was she still calling Juhyun at night? With no intention to agree or even talk about the incident? As Juhyun's voice went back and forth between cynicism and sympathy, what was Haesoo trying to hear?

Sure, Haesoo. Maybe this isn't a big deal. Maybe years from now you'll look back and think, Yeah, that was just something that happened. I don't know. But I don't want you to remember this period in your life with regret. What would be the point of wishing you had done this or that? Don't do anything you'll regret. That's all I want to say. That's it.

It was the same thing Juhyun had said the night before.

Haesoo did not ask how much more time had to pass before she would be able to say, "Yeah, that happened."

Casual catching up, open sharing of feelings, occasional bursts of laughter—Haesoo found these things missing from their conversations. Tripping, stalling, and lurching at the incident, their conversations stopped again and again. There was no moving around it.

Maybe Sei's conflict with her friends is similar, Haesoo thinks now. Maybe they just cannot get to a middle ground.

Haesoo wants to hear the child's story.

Why does she seem nervous every time the phone buzzes and a message comes up? Why does she look so scared? What demands and pressures are weighing on her?

You don't have dodgeball practice on Saturdays? Haesoo asks.

Sometimes I do, sometimes I don't. There's a practice today, but I skipped it.

Why?

Because. My legs hurt and I'm tired. And we have to rescue Turnip.

Haesoo nods, pretending not to see the blue-green bruise on her ankle. Just then, a small shadow appears in the distance. It's Kami. A little while later, a yellow creature emerges from behind the ginkgo tree.

Auntie, over there. Turnip, Sei whispers. It's Turnip. Haesoo slowly gets up. As always, Kami leads the way and Turnip limps after her. Turnip cannot fully open his eyes. His tongue rolls out and his head swings from side to side, almost knocking into the ground. It's clear he cannot help it. It's clear that some pain, some torment is jerking him around like a marionette.

Yes, I really hope we rescue him today, Haesoo says to herself.

Kami walks straight into the trap without thinking twice and does not flinch at the sound of the door shutting as she feasts. Then she lays down for a nap. What is Turnip learning from Kami's actions? If you are reckless, you will get caught? That getting caught isn't the worst thing in the world? Was it Kami's plan to secretly help Haesoo in this way?

On Sunday morning, Haesoo goes to the ginkgo tree lot by herself. Something amazing happens. Just after noon, Turnip comes to her. He's limping, but he comes straight toward her without hesitation. Turnip knows who she is. Turnip recognizes her. She is sure of it.

Haesoo works up the courage to reach out. Turnip touches the tip of her finger with his nose. He licks the Churu straight from her hands.

Have you changed your mind? Are you going to go into the trap today without a fight?

As Haesoo talks, Turnip looks her in the eye, opens his mouth a little, and makes a sound. It's more of a raspy sigh than anything else. Still, he seems to be doing better today than yesterday. His tongue isn't hanging out, and he isn't hanging his head so much.

What's going on? What happened?

But this is wishful thinking on her part. Turnip's fur is matted and caked all over. His swollen face is covered in tear boogers and streaks, and his body is astoundingly scrawny. He is such a mess that he almost looks dead as he is. It wouldn't be surprising if he fell over and died right this minute.

Haesoo looks into Turnip's deep amber eyes. His small paws, pointy ears, and wispy tail catch her eye in turn. The subtle rise and fall of his body with each breath. Turnip seems to have grown since she first saw him, to be getting closer to adult-hood. Even in pain, he seems faithful to his duty of surviving.

Haesoo decides to be brave. She tries to lure him to the trap. She distracts him by waving a long branch and pets Kami, who shows up a little later, which relaxes Turnip. Haesoo is desper-ately waiting for some pivotal moment. When that moment comes, she will grab Turnip and put him in the trap. She will grab that frail little creature with sheer force to rescue him.

But that doesn't happen.

Of course it doesn't. Turnip only paces around the yellow drop trap. Haesoo creeps up on him and tries to push him in. The second her hand touches him, he springs in the air. In an instant, he morphs into a jumpy, wild, strong cat. Turnip's claws come out and he growls; his canines are bared.

When Haesoo comes toward Turnip with the blanket she brought, he flees. Without giving Kami so much as a signal, he dashes off to the other side of the ginkgo tree.

Haesoo comes home before dusk. She doesn't wash up or eat before dozing off on the sofa. The house is so quiet that it feels deserted—a perfect place to fall asleep. But she cannot sleep deeply. A certain ambient, chattering noise keeps her trapped between consciousness and sleep.

Haesoo is in a dream bustling with people. They call her name and wave at her. She says hello to them and exchanges greetings. The people are somewhat familiar and somewhat not. Each time she turns around, people become less familiar. When she looks again, she does not recognize a single face. She pushes her way through the crowd of utterly strange faces in search of someone she knows. When she finally finds someone, she doesn't have a full view of their face because the head is bowed, but Haesoo knows. This is a person she knows well. She has known this person for a long time. She wedges herself through the packed-in crowd.

At last, Haesoo calls the person's name. The person turns to look at her. A face she has never seen, never thought she would see, a look so strange and indecipherable, a frighteningly harsh, final expression gazes straight at her.

Haesoo wakes up several times from these dreams. Past a certain point, she cannot go back to sleep anymore. The night wears on. She watches a television show as she chews on small bits of cheese and shriveled, wrinkly almonds.

This is all well and good, but we have got to get everyone together and talk about this.

We need to hear what the kids have to say, says the man on the television.

Wearing pajamas with blue stripes, he's sitting on the floor talking to a woman who appears to be his wife.

Why should I? Why do I have to hear what the kids have to say? I'm done listening to them. Really. Children never listen to their parents. I can't do this. I can't do this anymore.

The woman at the dressing table dabbing lotion on her face does not look at the man. The man's eyes are fixed on one spot on the floor as he kneads his foot. In the small room furnished with an old-fashioned closet, a small dresser, a dressing table, and a floor lamp, a heavy silence settles in. The man starts to say something. Resentment and disappointment, sympathy and frustration notwithstanding, the husband tries to persuade the wife. That is the role he has been given.

But his acting is incomparably forced. He overthinks his role as the husband in this scene. Or maybe that's just Haesoo's impression. Maybe the unflattering makeup on him? The costume that doesn't match the set dressing? Something personal happening in the actor's life that the viewers don't know about?

Scene change.

The man is sitting in a diner with a low ceiling talking to two people who appear to be husband and wife. They sit across from the man in matching aprons. Silence falls over the table when the man stops talking. All three look obliquely away from each other.

You know how your mother is, the man says assuredly after a long pause. She never lets things go. You have nothing to worry about. Just don't say a word about it. Turn a blind eye. Come by the house this Sunday. I have a plan. He eats a piece of *tteokbokki*. The man's acting is awkward in this scene as well. The lines of dialogue flow uninterruptedly among the characters, but the words come out mechanically and scatter in the air. These aren't words that can accompany gestures, sympathy, and encouragement to draw out others' words in turn. These are words that do not communicate.

As the man walks out of the diner, he mutters, Rock and a hard place. How did I end up in this position? Life gets tougher as I go, for crying out loud. How can I breathe when I can't get so much as a day's relief from this? I can't breathe, not one breath.

Haesoo repeats the man's lines out loud. This is an old show. She has seen it many times before. For some of the scenes, she can recite the lines exactly from memory. The man's role in this show is not a substantial one. In the fifty-minute episode, he appears maybe three or four times. So why does Haesoo remember his tone and expression, lines and gestures so accurately?

The actor, who is in his fifties, is playing the part of an old man in his seventies. He is just barely playing the role that's dragging him around. The first time she saw the show, Haesoo thought he was simply not a good actor. That he had foolishly taken on a role he couldn't handle, that he couldn't tell the difference between what he could or could not do.

Now, she has no thoughts regarding this man. No judgment, no criticism. She hits the off button on the remote. The screen goes dark with a flash, and the nondescript face of the man is wiped clean from Haesoo's memory.

∽

To Mr. Kyungjin Choi:

Hello,

I am sorry, it's been several weeks since I told you that I would give my answer regarding the suit against reporter Seong-mok Lee. I apologize for the late reply and hope you understand.

I have received your email. I understand all parties except for three will be pressing charges. I will keep in mind that gathering and sorting through evidence can take a great deal of time.

I should also tell you that I've been getting together with Seung-pyo Lee and Sujin Jang for the past few months. They're the only two people who came in for a consultation with me. I'm sure you remember. We don't get together with a specific purpose in mind, and definitely not on a regular basis. We talk for an hour, two hours tops. We catch up on each other's lives over coffee and go home.

There are moments when I—and they as well—feel starved for empathy and understanding. Talking to them makes me feel a little better.

Would it be okay if I mulled over Seong-mok Lee's case for a little longer? I think I need more time. I will let you know by the end of the month at the latest.

I'm sorry if I'm making things difficult for you. If there's anything I need to be informed of, please contact me anytime. I will do the same. And there's one more thing I would like to ask

Haesoo gets ready and leaves the house.

This is her first visit to town in nearly two months. She gets in the car and presses the start button. The engine turns over smoothly. She pulls out of the alley and gradually speeds up. The fact that she is driving away from her house calms her heart. With both hands on the steering wheel and her back straight, she keeps her eyes on the wide, open road. The tall buildings, flashing billboards, and throngs of people rushing by catch her eye.

Haesoo rolls down the window a bit. The light, air, and noise flowing in feel strange. They belong entirely to the outside. They put her mind at ease.

Haesoo walks toward the table by the window, and the familiar face gets up to greet her. Seung-pyo Lee, a man in his early thirties. Haesoo sees him once every month or two. He is one of the contemptible people who drove a person to death with his injudicious, reckless remarks.

The summit of the contemptibles.

A window seat at a café is perhaps not a suitable place for them to congregate and scheme. Or perhaps there is no better place for them to feel shame and learn what it is to be insulted.

Hi, good to see you. Sujin is running late.

Seung-pyo looks better than he did last time. He's gained some weight and the color in his face has improved. Haesoo sits across from him. The soft classical music playing in the café ends and a lively jazz number starts up.

I still come across people who recognize me, he says. But no one mistreats me like before. That's an improvement. I'm grateful for that.

Seung-pyo sips his coffee and keeps looking over his shoulder. He was an average guy in his thirties with an office job. He's still a guy with an office job, but no longer average. The way people look at him, the way he looks at people, his company. The dynamics with the people he works with. His life was downgraded. And he is at least capable of admitting that he brought it upon himself.

He has forgotten how to return to who he was. He has lost his past self. Same goes for Haesoo. This is the biggest thing they have in common. They must reconcile with the life they face in the present. They must find a way.

Sujin Jang is twenty minutes late. She is a woman in her forties who runs a large online shopping site. Her business is on the verge of bankruptcy.

The conversation takes off now that all three are present.

First thing I do every morning is log onto the website and erase all the troll comments. You know what I'm talking about? One time, someone posted where my son Hanbin goes to school. He's ten. What did he ever do to anyone? Remember I told you last time that someone keyed my car? I've been parking far away from the house since then, but somehow they still find it and wreck it. I put the cover on recently and found it slashed with a knife the next day.

Seung-pyo looks grim as he listens to Sujin. He worries this might happen to him as well.

Seung-pyo leans across the table and says, So, what happens if we sue? Will everyone who posted malicious comments be punished? Won't they just get slapped with a small fine? And who decides what constitutes a malicious comment? His voice grows softer. I've been doing some research, and everyone had a different answer.

Seung-pyo, listen to me. It doesn't matter what constitutes a malicious comment. Our goal is to make sure they stop writing them. How much longer are you going to let them kick you around? Honestly, I thought I could just suck it up. Ignore it. But there is no end to this. How can people be so unrelenting? It simply blows my mind. If we keep taking it like we are now, this will not end. Not unless we do something. I have to do something for Hanbin's sake, if nothing else. What did he ever do to deserve this? Am I wrong?

Sujin leans across the table too. Seung-pyo and Sujin's heads nearly touch. Haesoo thinks Sujin has changed.

The three of them met a year ago, at Haesoo's lawyer's office. Joint response, preemptive action, countermeasures. They sat in an office that felt almost bare for its minimalist lack of furniture and discussed these topics. Terms that are no more than abstractions. Like coming across a word for the first time in a dictionary. Expressions Haesoo never used in her life and never had to. She sat in a daze as the words floated around her.

Could we talk? It'll take just a moment. Sujin had approached Haesoo after the meeting. She was waiting for the elevator. Seung-pyo, who was pacing nervously a few steps away from them, followed.

What do you think? Have you decided what to do? Youngjin Choi? Or Kyungjin? Who introduced you to this lawyer? A close friend? Can you trust them? I'm sorry. I'm bombarding you with questions and we just met. I'm guessing today was your first meeting with the lawyer? With Mr. Youngjin Choi, I mean, Kyungjin?

Sujin's words came out rapid fire as she beat her iced coffee with a straw. Seung-pyo took in every word with a blank expression. Haesoo felt that they were frightened. Unmistakably. Just as Haesoo was. That day, the three of them shared a sense of fear and terror. They were entering a tragic period in their lives that was already beginning to cast a shadow. Or perhaps this was just a conversation that three fools who made a ridiculous mistake might share.

Still, Haesoo remembers everything. When she parted ways with the other two and left the office, what caught her eye was not the tall buildings and the roads stretching to the horizon, nor the scenes of the city bustling with cars and people. She saw something she had never seen before: the mouth of a cave holding its breath, lying in wait over the background of the bustling, lively scenery. The horrifyingly blackout before a scene change.

But now, Haesoo no longer detects fear in Sujin.

What's going on with you, Dr. Lim? Did the trolls stop posting things on the counseling center message board? Is the website still down and all that mess? Has anyone tried to contact you directly? She pauses, then says, Several times a day, I think I should just change my number. But I have buyers and I have regulars, so it's not an easy decision. By the way, did you change your number, Seung-pyo? Not yet, huh?

Haesoo tells her that she has not heard from the counseling center. Then she changes the subject. She tells them that she's been trying to rescue a cat.

Cat? Like a cat that lives in the streets? Why are you trying to rescue a cat?

To take it to the vet. It's not doing well.

Oh, to get it fixed up. That's nice of you. I didn't know you were interested in that kind of thing. Seung-pyo, have you made up your mind? The lawyer said you can sue them for defamation.

Sujin's focus quickly returns to Seung-pyo and they go back in time again.

Ugh, I don't know what to do. I looked it up online, and it's apparently not easy to stick the trolls with a charge. I don't know if I want to risk dredging things up by suing them. You know I've been postponing the wedding since last year. I really need to set a date. My parents are nagging me and my fiancée is getting anxious.

Seung-pyo, listen carefully. Do you think it'll get better if you continue to lay low like this? How much longer are you going to live with your legs and arms bound? This is no way to live. We are as good as dead. Can you keep living like this? Can you?

Of course not. I can't keep going like this. But I don't know what choice I have. I don't know what the right decision is.

Sujin and Seung-pyo's conversation goes around in circles. If someone were to overhear them, what would they think it was about? Would they come off as victims? As perpetrators? Perpetrators posing as victims? Victims disguised as perpetrators?

Have you given it more thought, Dr. Lim? Seung-pyo asks. Have you reached a decision? He wants to know if Haesoo is going to sit by and watch as people post libelous comments, spread lies, and attack her maliciously and continuously. The words and sentences are different, but he's asking the same questions as the lawyer.

Haesoo changes the subject. The days are getting warmer. This summer is going to be very hot. There's a hurricane coming at the end of the month. Then she finally says what she came to say.

I'm sorry. I won't be able to meet with you for the time being. I hope you end up doing what's best for you.

Seung-pyo, who was gathering up the cups to put them away, meets her eye and asks, What? Why not? Did you talk with the lawyer? Does that mean you won't be taking any action? Why not? Are you sure that's what you want to do? Do you know something I don't know? If you know something, you have to tell me, Dr. Lim.

Doing nothing can be a choice. In some cases it is a tougher decision than taking action. But Haesoo stops herself from saying as much. That isn't the reason she came to this decision. This is not so much a decision as a postponement.

Instead, Haesoo wipes the water on the table with a napkin as she says, I just need more time. I'm kind of distracted at the moment, too. I don't have the space to think about other things. Because I have to rescue this cat.

Haesoo says goodbye and heads straight to the parking garage. She gets in the car, puts on her seatbelt, and starts the engine. It's time for her to go home. She fights off the urge to look back.

The ginkgo tree lot becomes something of a place of worship to Haesoo.

The time she spends there waiting for Turnip brings her calm. She does not know where this calm and peace are coming from. Sometimes she stays past sundown, until darkness settles in. Sometimes she forgets that she is waiting for Turnip.

When she looks up, she watches the ginkgo tree above her. She is often transfixed by the green of the leaves that are becoming alarmingly vivid. She sometimes makes a tall stack of flat rocks or gathers branches to build a tower. She enjoys knocking down her careful constructions with one flick of her finger.

With everything, building is hard but destroying is easy.

If life is carefully stacking one block after another, taking just one of those blocks away can make the whole thing tumble. Maybe that's the lesson she's learning right now. She is shocked at the ubiquity of parables all around her.

Turnip makes an appearance from time to time.

Keeping a wary eye on his surroundings, he eats and drinks his fill, makes eye contact with Haesoo, and sometimes comes up close and meows at her. Turnip is sleepy in the morning, exhausted in the afternoon, and a bit more energetic at night. Haesoo doesn't know what Turnip does in the small hours of the morning or where he goes.

But it's clear that Turnip recognizes her. There is a cautious yet sure bond between Turnip and Haesoo, which can't be found in friendly Kami, who makes eye contact and rubs her cheek against anyone. Turnip demonstrates this bond in a very subtle way.

When Haesoo beckons Turnip during the day, he stares at her before he touches the tip of her finger with his nose. The cats' greeting. The standoffish, coolness of it. Turnip looks up at her and makes a faint noise as he paces around her. When he's in a good mood, he sniffs around her shoes.

But Haesoo is not relieved by these changes in Turnip. It makes her more nervous, and not just because of Turnip's limp, matted hair. The drool hanging off his soggy mouth. The eyes that sometimes close as if from pain shooting through his body like electricity.

Haesoo does not know what she feels toward Turnip. Pity for him? Or pity for herself? Perhaps a laughable sense of superiority as a human. She cannot understand why she is trying to rescue Turnip. She is at times amused by her own belief that she can save this poor little creature. What she confronts at the ginkgo tree lot is herself. She has never had a free moment from herself. Not one step away from herself.

One afternoon, she extends her hand toward exhausted Turnip dozing off. She is bold, as though guided by an unseen force. Turnip's fur is clumped in places, wet and slippery. When her hand grabs the scruff of his neck, his feral nature awakens.

He twists and kicks. One moment of doubt and this attempt will fail. Haesoo will never get another chance.

She grabs the scruff tighter and tries to hold down Turnip's small, scrawny body with her other hand. Then comes a moment that defies sequential description. It's horrific chaos—grabbing, flailing, hanging on, shaking, shouting, pleading, and cornering.

Haesoo grabs her overshirt sitting nearby, rolls it up into a ball, and tries to contain Turnip with it. She has the little thing pinned to the ground, and she is doing everything in her power to not give up. She opens the trap door with one foot and tries to shove Turnip inside. An incredible force explodes out of Turnip's little body. A cloud of dust flies up as he kicks. Spit flies everywhere. He screams.

By some miracle, she is able to push Turnip into the trap. No. That's what she thinks. Before she can even open the trap door, Turnip slips out of her grasp. Turnip keeps leaning to the side as he runs away, nearly hitting his head on the ground. He must be in shock.

Turnip, Turnip.

Haesoo gets up for a moment, then plops back on the ground. She's just as tired as the cat. Her arms and the backs of her hands are scratched and bloodied from his sharp claws. She wraps her mauled arm in her shirt. Blood soaks through the sheer fabric. Then she rushes away from the ginkgo tree lot.

Have you rescued Turnip? Oh, what happened to your arm? Are you okay?

Maru Mom is shocked at the sight of Haesoo, who brings both the drop trap and the metal trap later that evening. The milk distribution center with the shutter down has a pile of unopened mail sitting outside. Haesoo notices a for-rent sign down by the corner of the shutter that she hasn't seen before. It seems they've been out of business for some time.

I'm going to stop trying. I don't think this is something I can do.

Oh, no. Did you hurt yourself trying to rescue him? Is that how this happened, Maru Mom asks as she looks at the bandages patching up Haesoo's arm. Maru Mom is disappointed in Haesoo for giving up because a tiny, frail cat gave her a few scratches. Haesoo thinks she is. Or maybe Maru Mom has seen this coming.

Haesoo says, Even if I rescue him, I can't take responsibility. I've never looked after an animal in my life. And I wouldn't feel comfortable fixing him up and releasing him back into the streets. It's just not something I can take on. I'm sorry.

Haesoo looks down at the two traps she put on the ground. Then she offers Maru Mom a small paper bag of cookies she picked up at a nearby bakery. Maru Mom says thank you and Haesoo adds that the traps have been sanitized.

Okay, if that's what you've got to do. Did you clean your cuts? Have you been to the doctor yet? You will need a tetanus shot because they live in the streets. Definitely go see a doctor to be safe.

Maru Mom looks at Haesoo like she has something to say, then picks up the traps and the paper bag and turns to go. A few streets down, a siren grows loud and fades. Haesoo stands and watches as Maru Mom walks away, dragging her flip-flops.

To Mr. Hanseong Lee:

Hello, it's been a while.

I'm writing to ask you a favor. There is a client called Ju Hanna I was treating at the counseling center. She is a woman in her late twenties suffering from a chronic depression that comes in at intervals. I worked with her for over a year, and found that she has a strong drive to get better. I cannot give you the details of her case, but I would like you to refer her to a few therapists she might see instead. I think this small gesture of care is the least I can do for someone who placed her trust in me and the center.

And there is one more thing I would like to ask of you.

Regarding the questions that Ms. Jo Minyoung asked me during the final meeting to decide my future at the counseling center—I need to point out that they were inappropriate questions, which should not have been brought up at the meeting. I cannot help but think it was malicious of her to problematize my method and attitude as a therapist. As you know, my conduct was far from what she described. Even if the descriptions were accurate, they should not have been voiced at this meeting. Furthermore, Ms. Jo was the last person who should have been giving me such feedback.

Since the meeting was scheduled ahead of time, I would like to know what arrangements were made in advance. Was Ms. Jo prepped to ask the questions, or was she acting on her own? And how much did it end up influencing the decision of my termination?

I was given notice of termination, yet I don't know through what process this decision was reached. As the person who was dismissed, I believe I have the right to request information regarding the process. Unless I am given valid grounds for termination, I cannot accept your decision.

This is not an unreasonable request, and I do not have ulterior motives. I only

Haesoo stops and fixes a few word choices at the end. *Arrangements were made in advance* becomes *arrangements were made behind closed doors*, then *arrangements were secretly made*. *Prepped* is replaced with words like *conspire* and *scheme* and *plot*. The letter, an expressionless face, begins to take on a certain look. Emotions Haesoo has never been able to reveal. Inappropriate sentiments. Words that will bring on instant retribution.

Another letter she cannot send.

For an injured street cat, Turnip has left a pretty serious gash on the back of Haesoo's hand.

The next morning, she gets three stitches, a tetanus shot, and a shot of antibiotics. Red splotches cover her arm, swollen with uneven bumps. She looks like she has taken a beating. The doctor tells her that she needs a dressing change every other day. He instructs her not to get the cut wet.

At reception, where Haesoo waits for her prescription, the nurse asks, Would you like to make an appointment for your next visit? If you don't, you might have to wait a long time.

Okay. I'd like to come at a less busy time, please.

Two days from now? That's Thursday. I'll put you down for ten a.m.

A doctor's office on the second floor of a building without an elevator. She had not expected a run-down place like this to be packed with patients every day. She leaves the office and hurries across the hall and down the stairwell. An old woman slowly making her way down the steps with both hands holding on to the railing starts talking to her.

For heaven's sake, this place is so busy every day. Every time I come here, it takes two hours out of my day. I guess people are always getting sick. Hospitals never go through a recession. Sickness doesn't care how the economy is doing.

Haesoo does not reply, but the old woman goes on anyway: But this doctor is honest. And not a bad doctor, either. Why would people keep coming here if he isn't? Climbing up and

105

down all these stairs on my bad knees? Rest assured, he can fix most things with his eyes closed.

Haesoo nods goodbye and hurries out of the building.

Her fear of being recognized comes true one week later when she returns to the office and sits in the busy waiting room to get her stitches out.

Hi, fancy seeing you here! It's me. Do you remember?

Someone is trying to get her attention. A man sitting by the television. He's right across the oval table from Haesoo, who is sitting by the exit.

Haesoo's expression says she can't place him.

The brick house in the back there, the man says. You're that therapist. Right?

The man comes over, determined. The people on the sofa lean out of the way to make room for him. Who is this man? Friend or foe? Just an onlooker? Indifferent eyes in the room turn back to the television.

Haesoo's heart pounds. A hot rush of blood spreads over her face. She puts down the magazine she was looking at and sits up straight.

I haven't seen you around in so long. I thought you'd moved. Do you still live around here?

What brings you to the doctor's? Did you hurt your hand? Oh no, what happened?

It's okay. It's almost healed now, she responds cautiously. With just the right amount of body language. With a blank expression that reveals neither amity nor hostility. The man keeps talking, habitually clenching and opening his fist. His hands are large and heavy. His thick, rounded fingernails are filthy around the edges. The moment the missing tip of his pinky catches her eye, she realizes who he is.

A few winters ago, the handyman had come to her house after a pipe had burst in the cold. He came on his red scooter loaded with all sorts of equipment and parts, inspected the house inside and out, and found the exact spot where the pipe froze and burst with his water leak detector. Sweat poured as he dug up the frozen earth and replaced the pipe in the yard. He dug up the ground, replaced the meter, installed a new pipe, and paved it neatly with cement in just a few hours.

Oh, I've been meaning to say something, if I ever ran into you. Just hear me out. Don't think of it as sticking my nose in your business. Those people who're cussing you out and bullying you on the internet—I hear you're suing them? I saw the news on the internet, I think today or yesterday?

He must be talking about Sujin and Seung-pyo. Or is it about someone else? Are people still interested in that incident? Countless comments had driven that man to his death, and Haesoo was one of the few people revealed as the source of one of those comments.

Yes, that's right, Haesoo replies. She cannot tell yet if the words are coming from a hostile place.

Words burst out of the man as if he can barely contain them. Listen, I know how you feel. One hundred percent. This has been going on forever, and I understand you're upset. But a man died. Nothing good will come of this for you. People will just call you shameless. People say all kinds of nonsense when they don't know what's what. That's just how it is. Best to lay low. You have no other choice but to play dead and wait until it blows over.

What does this man think he knows? What about his words does he believe is distinct from anybody else's?

Don't take it the wrong way, the man says. I'm only saying this because we live in the same neighborhood and we've met a few times. I wouldn't say this to a total stranger. I wouldn't waste my breath.

The man's overly hushed voice stirs curiosity in the room. Peering eyes turn toward Haesoo. Looking down at the spread of magazines on the table, she searches for words. Maybe she needs a new language. Maybe she finds herself frequently at a loss for words due to the confines of her mother tongue.

She feels trapped in the meanings and contexts expanding without end, in the words distorting and overlapping. In the vocabulary of the mother tongue that never refers to one thing only. She might be able to find something like a rebuttal with the right words and a fresh sentence structure if she were given a new language.

In the meantime, the man goes on and on. An old woman on the other side of the room chides, Excuse me. Could you keep it down? We're all not feeling well. This is not a place for chatter.

Chatter? I'm talking quietly. Who're you calling loud? What good is it to act all proper and pretend nothing is happening?

We're all neighbors. We should offer helpful advice in times of trouble. Standing by with your mouth shut when your neighbor's house is on fire doesn't help anyone.

How is sticking your nose in someone else's business "advice"? the old woman replies. You're saying that for your own benefit.

My benefit? How does this benefit me? You better watch what you say, lady.

Watch what I say? You're the one who isn't watching himself. You're the one running your mouth when everyone else is keeping quiet.

The old woman shows no sign of backing down. A few more people join in the discussion, adding details and rigor. This is the last thing Haesoo wants. They toss around words like *mistake* and *forgiveness*, *repentance* and *suicide*, *justice* and *accusation*, *damages* and *innocence*. They invoke the names of famous politicians and celebrities now dead and gone.

Haesoo looks toward the exam room. She wishes the nurse would come through the door and call her name. But it won't be her turn for a while.

She sits like someone waiting for her verdict. Like people she has seen seated at the defendant's table—a little hunched, head bowed, shoving down the words and feelings that are tearing their way up, awaiting the sentencing handed down by public opinion that is as unpredictable and merciless as the raging sea.

She makes a fist and gives her stitched-up hand a firm squeeze. She feels a deep, jolting pain. She presses harder, resolved to focus on the simple, straightforward pain on her skin. Resolved not to be tossed about by the words shooting through her without mercy.

Then why don't we ask the person herself? someone says, cutting off the conversation and looking at Haesoo. Why argue among ourselves when we can just ask?

Are they giving her a chance to defend herself? Are they asking if she has any last words? She wants to show how nervous she is, to let the trembling, indisputably emotional words pour out. She wants to ramble on and show them what they want to see. What they want to hear.

Haesoo does not say a word.

She does not ask if they are taking pleasure in prodding at the humiliation of an exposed person from all angles while keeping their own shameful parts hidden safely behind words like *ethics* and *justice*. Haesoo is aware that she is not innocent of these faults.

Haesoo Lim! Haesoo Lim, the doctor will see you now.

The exam door opens at last and the nurse calls her name. She jumps to her feet and leaves the waiting room.

A few days later, in the evening, the intercom rings.

Darkness fills the intercom screen. There is a broken light by the door. Long ago, Haesoo had argued with Taeju when he tried to change the bulb. She wanted to get a new light.

Replace the one that radiates dim yellow light with a sensor-activated floodlight.

Haesoo realizes that she has long forgotten about this. She is struck by how few people now visit this house that she hadn't thought about the lamp for a long time.

Who is it? Haesoo asks, and a wisp of a voice calls back, Auntie, Auntie. It's me, Sei.

Haesoo opens the door to find the child with a ball under one arm. Sei's face is glistening with sweat.

I was going to text you, but my phone is broken. I dropped it in the toilet. Auntie, aren't you going to rescue Turnip anymore?

Haesoo catches a whiff of spicy sauce. She looks down at Sei's duffle bag with the strap so extended that it drags on the ground.

No, she answers. I'm going to stop. I don't think I can anymore. I'm sorry I didn't tell you sooner.

Why not? Why can't you rescue him anymore?

Well, I don't think I'm cut out for it. I don't think Turnip wants to be rescued, either.

I heard that you hurt your hand. Maru Mom told me. She said you hurt yourself trying to catch Turnip. Are you okay?

Nothing to worry about. It's almost all better.

Haesoo gently waves the injured hand. The child does not turn to leave. She sways back and forth, glancing around her like she has something left to say.

Have you seen Turnip? Haesoo asks.

Yeah, I went to the lot and didn't see the trap. I've seen Turnip almost every day. I gave him some Churu yesterday, but he didn't eat much. I think his mouth hurts a lot.

Sei balances on one foot and removes the shoe from the other. Then she taps on it. Loose rocks and sand fall out and hit the ground. Haesoo doesn't want to continue the conversation. She isn't confident she can explain why her resolve to rescue Turnip has vanished like a mirage.

Haesoo changes the subject. Do you have dodgeball practice these days?

Yeah. Almost every day.

The question seems to have prodded some part of Sei. Her face crumbles. She looks like she wants to cry.

Did you come here straight from school? Have you had dinner? Your parents must be worried. Do you want to come in for a while?

The child does not hesitate or give much of an answer. She simply follows Haesoo inside the house.

Haesoo is worn out, tired, enervated. The cut on the back of her hand burns and her eyes sting from lack of sleep. She looks inside the refrigerator for something to eat. She hears Sei go into the bathroom. The sound of water running. The refrigerator is fully stocked with expired food. Vegetables and fruits have gone soft with rot in the produce drawer, and piles of leftovers in containers fill the shelves. Ready-to-eat meals, colorful bottles of condiments, an assortment of vitamins and supplements with ingredients and benefits she cannot recall. The testament of a woman who has lost her hunger.

Haesoo manages to salvage two tomatoes, three eggs, and a few slices of cheese. She hears the sound of the bathroom door opening. She pushes the food back into the refrigerator and calls to Sei, Would you like something to eat? Should we order in? I haven't had dinner yet, either. Why don't we call your parents first to let them know?

Sei yells back from the bathroom, Okay. I can call them later!

The pizza arrives quickly. Sei and Haesoo sit side by side on the sofa. The pizza isn't all that special, but the dough is still warm and the strong flavor of the sauce stirs Haesoo's appetite. The child scarfs down her slice as Haesoo watches from the corner of her eye and takes small bites.

Sei seems more tan. Maybe she has lost weight. Haesoo turns on the television and turns down the volume. A close-up of people clapping and laughing appears.

Auntie, I've had this pizza before. When I went to the department store with Mom. It tastes exactly the same.

Really? Then we should have tried something else.

The tension lifts from the child's face. She gingerly pushes the bit of cheese stuck by her lip into her mouth and mumbles, No, that was a long time ago. When I was really little. I don't live with Mom anymore. I can only see her once a month. But I didn't get to see her last month, or the month before that. She's busy. She always says she's busy.

Yeah? You must be disappointed, Haesoo answers as she pops a slice of pickle in her mouth. She isn't surprised. She doesn't ask Sei more questions. She doesn't want to appear sympathetic or sad for her. The child is once again preoccupied with pizza. Should Haesoo be glad that she has become fully accustomed to the ever more surprising stories that people divulge? Is the child thrown by Haesoo's unmoved reaction? Or somewhat relieved?

Haesoo's matter-of-fact response opens up the child. She tells her more. Like a pebble tossed on the still surface of a lake, the child's words send slow, gentle ripples out until they encircle them both.

I haven't even been to Mom's house. She promised she would take me, but now she's saying she can't. I don't even know her address. If I know her address, I can see her house. With the street view. You know, Auntie. The internet map.

Haesoo nods as she changes the channel. She flips through them quickly. There's nothing on that a child might like. She stops at a channel showing a herd of elephants crossing a plain and turns up the volume.

Your mother must have her reasons. Give her time, is all Haesoo says. When she offers to get Sei another slice of pizza, the child says, That's okay. I can do it.

Sei grabs another slice carefully so the toppings don't fall off and returns her focus to chewing and swallowing. She keeps glancing up at Haesoo with a concerned look. This is oddly consoling to Haesoo.

I used to live in this house with my husband. Until recently. But we live separately now. Some people are better apart than together.

The words flow out of her.

But why? Sei asks.

Because some people hurt each other when they're together. It's very hard on both people.

Auntie, is it nicer living separately? Really better? Sei asks, eating a piece of green bell pepper. In this moment, she doesn't seem like a kid, but an old woman who can see right through Haesoo. She picks apart the word "nice" for the meanings it encompasses. Easy. Convenient. Effortless. Calm. Quiet. Peaceful. What Haesoo thought when she was parting ways with Taeju. The values she leaned on. Haesoo does not mention what hides soundlessly like shadows behind these words. Cowardice. Quitting. Loneliness. Solitude. Total collapse.

I don't know, she finally answers. Time will tell for sure, don't you think?

See, it's not all good, the child answers, pleased with herself.

What do you call this kind of exchange? The kind of unobstructed communication Haesoo has not experienced for a while and believed she never would again? There are no obstacles standing between her and Sei when they talk. The conversation moves forward, takes smooth turns, and skates freely through their hearts. Words open the unyielding door within, reach deep into each other, and draw up more words that genuinely mirror who they are.

Words without artifice. Without cumbersome decorations. Without design, subtext, ill-will. Words that have never been expressed. Words curled up inside, yet to take shape or color.

Auntie, during dodgeball practice today, I really wanted to just leave and go home. The other kids kept telling me that I was hit. But I really wasn't hit. Sori kept yelling that the ball touched my hair. There's this girl called Sori Yu. Everybody loves Sori. They don't even listen to me.

That must have made you feel bad. Do you think Sori saw wrong?

No. She said the same thing last time and the time before that.

Do you think Sori is doing that on purpose? What do you think?

Sei takes a bite of pepperoni and looks up at her. Haesoo refills Sei's cup of cola and says she doesn't have to answer if she doesn't want to. It's clear that the child is distressed.

Auntie, can you just listen? Without saying anything?

Of course, Haesoo answers. I can just listen.

The conversation grows deeper and wider. Distrust and fear are pushed back as it expands its perimeter. Haesoo might even say that a light has turned on in the child. Haesoo feels they are really seeing each other now. How much does the child's heart mirror her own? How different is the child's world from hers? Haesoo occasionally forgets that the person she's talking to is a child barely ten years old.

Auntie, about Turnip—can't you try to rescue him just one more time? Sei asks as she steps out of Haesoo's gate. Raindrops are starting to fall. Haesoo grabs two umbrellas and hands one to Sei.

If you rescue Turnip, I can adopt him, Sei says. I'll talk to Dad. He said no, but when he sees Turnip, he might change his mind.

Do you think so?

Yes. Because Turnip is really cute when you see him.

Okay. Let's give it some thought, Haesoo replies, holding up Sei's umbrella, which keeps slipping as she looks at Haesoo.

One week passes, and Thursday returns.

Haesoo promised that she would try to rescue Turnip just one more time, but that was never going to be the deal. She's been standing vigil by the ginkgo tree lot for the last four days. With the two traps from Maru Mom set up on the path, she sits a good distance away and waits for Turnip to show. Sei comes straight to the lot after dodgeball practice.

Sometimes she runs over completely out of breath, and other times she sneaks up and scares Haesoo. She gives her candy and caramel squares she got from who knows where.

The days grow increasingly hot. The thick blanket of heat does not lift until long past noontime.

The waiting flows by quietly. But there are moments of levity and joy as well. Haesoo watches as Sei bounces the ball by herself. Sometimes Haesoo passes the ball back and forth, or throws it really hard at Sei as Sei instructs.

Today, Sei has brought a ball that is smaller than a volleyball. It's a cushy orange ball with a bumpy surface.

Auntie, throw this at me. From over there. You have to hit me.

With this ball? Haesoo asks.

I can duck better if I practice with a smaller ball. Hurry!

Haesoo throws the ball as instructed, picks it up when Sei throws it back, and scrambles after it when it rolls away. Haesoo begins to sweat. If someone were to see her like this, what would they say? A villain enjoying her day without any regard for the tragedy she brought upon another person? A brazen woman with a heart of stone?

But this moment is only this moment. It is not the result, cause, or reason for anything that has happened in her past. This moment is a moment that cannot be explained in terms of cause and effect. Time does not flow in a straight line, and neither do the moments in a life. Just as she cannot go through life with just one face.

Perhaps this is what Haesoo is learning as she plays catch with Sei. Or perhaps this is what the child is teaching her.

Turnip sometimes shows up in the late afternoons, and other times timidly shows himself as Haesoo and Sei are packing up to go. Kami is always with him. Whenever it is, Haesoo and Sei stop whatever they're doing and keep a watchful eye on the cats.

One night, around dusk, Turnip appears. The game of catch stops. "Game of catch" may not be the right way to put it. Haesoo is aware that this is the child's desperate fight for survival.

Auntie, do you see that? On Turnip's mouth? I looked it up on the internet, and they say it's stomatitis. Cats get that a lot. He might have to get all of his teeth pulled, too.

Turnip looks up at Sei as she bounces the ball in place and, without taking his eyes off of her, makes his way to the food bowl. Kami waits her turn behind Turnip, who swallows the kibble. A flock of crows caw in the ginkgo tree.

A wait without end. An attempt guaranteed to fail the moment resignation sets in.

Haesoo realizes that she is once again involved in an impossible plan. It seems what Haesoo and Sei are doing has nothing to do with rescuing a poor cat living on the streets.

But exactly two days later, Turnip is rescued. Late one afternoon, Sei catches Turnip. Haesoo has gone to use the bathroom in the nearby convenience store and is returning with two cans of cold drinks when Sei, who was standing guard in the lot, comes running. She gestures at Haesoo to be quiet by holding one finger to her lip and waves at her with her free hand.

Auntie, Auntie. Are you ready for this? The child whispers with uncontained excitement on her face.

What? Ready for what? What happened?

Sei points at the trap under the tree. The trap is covered with a large blanket. Auntie, I rescued Turnip. I caught him, Sei whispers.

Really? Did you really?

It's true. Haesoo goes over to the trap and lifts the blanket. Turnip is curled in a tight ball with his ears folded back flat. He snarls and bares his fangs. Just as Sei said, Turnip's mouth is in bad shape. The swelling in his gums makes it impossible for the cat to close his mouth all the way. The drool from his mouth has soaked his chest, and his white and ginger fur has turned ashen. Kami is curled up next to Turnip, stretching her legs and pawing playfully. Her soft little pink paw pads come in and out of view.

How did you do it? How did you get them? Did you hurt yourself?

No, I didn't get hurt at all. I got Kami in the trap, and then Turnip tried to go in, too. When Turnip was a little bit inside, I pushed him the rest of the way with the blanket. Pretty good, right?

Sei's voice is full of confidence. She sounds like she wants to gloat a little. How did such a magical thing happen? How did a thing that seems so impossible suddenly happen? Haesoo cannot believe Sei's words.

Auntie, can you believe it? Isn't it amazing? Really super amazing?

I can hardly believe it! That was super amazing of you. Well done, she says to the child.

The vet's office has a floor-to-ceiling window in the waiting room that looks onto the street. There's an unobstructed view outside-in and inside-out. When Haesoo and Sei walk into the waiting room with the metal trap, people have already begun to corral their rambling dogs.

Is this your first visit here? asks the receptionist. When Haesoo says yes, there are follow-up questions. Then she asks for the names and symptoms of the cats.

Turnip! Turnip and Kami, Sei answers. The ginger one is Turnip and the black one is Kami. Turnip is the one that's sick. I think he's hurt his mouth really bad.

The receptionist comes around to the front and looks inside the trap. Then she gives Haesoo an uneasy look. It seems she is not happy about this difficult patient's visit. The receptionist asks a few more routine questions, tells them to wait, and disappears into the back.

Haesoo and Sei wrap the trap in a blanket, put it down on the floor, and wait for the receptionist to come back. An awkward, uncomfortable silence surrounds them. It seems they are not welcome here. People peer at Haesoo, Sei, and the trap. One dog totters toward them and sniffs around the trap. Someone quickly snatches the dog back, but it flails, trying to free itself from the owner's grasp. The dog whimpers and barks, which makes another dog bark, and soon the waiting room is full of the sound of dogs barking.

Is it a street cat? asks the vet when he comes to the reception desk at last.

Yes.

The vet comes around to the front and lifts the blanket to look inside. A blank expression. Gestures of only the most basic politeness.

The vet lifts his head and says, I'm afraid it will be difficult to treat it here. It has a serious case of stomatitis. I think you'll have better luck at a clinic that specializes in cats.

Is there such a clinic?

Our clinic mostly treats dogs.

Where could I find one near here?

Well, I'm not sure.

Haesoo and Sei leave with the trap. The child is out of words. She only looks up at Haesoo with nervous eyes.

Haesoo pulls out her phone and looks for another vet who will treat Turnip. Only after she has made an appointment and they begin to walk down the street does Sei break her silence. They treat animals that are not sick but refuse to help Turnip who is really sick? They're so annoying. Stuck-up jerks. Morons. Freaking dumbheads. When her eyes meet Haesoo's, she looks away. Was that anger, fear, or a momentary feeling that rushed up? Or something that has been hiding quietly inside her for a long time?

Turnip will be fine. You don't need to worry anymore, Haesoo says, pretending not to see the tears about to fall from Sei's eyes.

Haesoo and Sei arrive at the vet's office just in time for their appointment. The small waiting room is crowded but surprisingly quiet. People keep their distance from each other and don't seem interested in Haesoo and Sei. They appear grim and serious. Perhaps they don't have the luxury of being distracted. Are they coming face to face with the reality of the usually abstract ideas of life and death, loss and parting? The tense atmosphere makes Haesoo nervous. She shifts her posture and sits up straight.

Turnip, we're ready for you.

At last, it's Haesoo and Sei's turn. They pick up the trap and go into the exam room.

Let's have a look.

The vet in thick glasses sets the trap down on the exam table and slowly lifts the blanket. The two cats come into view one after the other. Turnip is curled up against the far end of the trap, and Kami seems a little scared. The long, narrow trap is too small for two cats, but they don't seem uncomfortable in there. Perhaps because they're still small. On second thought, Haesoo sees that Kami is much larger than Turnip.

The doctor puts on gloves, opens the trap door, and reaches in. Without a hint of hesitation. Haesoo averts her eyes, but nothing happens. Both Turnip and Kami behave.

Let's see. Let's get this one out first, the vet says in a whisper as he pulls Kami deftly from the trap. Kami stretches and rubs her cheek against the vet's hand.

This kid is very fond of people. Why don't you wait here for a moment? he says to Kami. The problem's the other one. Turnip's his name? Turnip, let me have a look at you. It's okay. I'm just going to look. Oh, you poor thing. That must have hurt.

Turnip's eyes keep closing. He is nearly debilitated from fighting the onslaught of terror. He hardly has the energy to show his fangs and threaten the vet.

Has Turnip been eating okay? It can't be easy to eat in this condition.

Sei answers, Churu is Turnip's favorite food in the world. But he's had a hard time eating Churu lately. He used to eat a bit of kibble, but now he just spits it all out. By shaking his head like this. Like he's having a seizure.

That's because his mouth hurts. I think he's hurt his front paw here, too. Do you know when he hurt his paw?

It wasn't so bad at first. When I saw him in the winter for the first time.

Last winter? Would you happen to remember exactly when that was?

Um, I think it was near Christmas. I mean, around Christmas.

The vet examines Turnip this way and that. Every new touch reveals a clear view of his hidden wounds. The swelling at the back of the ear is about to burst, and the flattened front paw is matted with fur. There are fine scratches on his nose that have healed.

What do you think happened to him? Haesoo asks.

Well, it could have been a territorial fight between the cats, or it could have been a person. The paw looks like it was stuck in a trap somewhere. This happens sometimes. People who don't like cats will do anything to drive them out.

Sei instantly objects, Why? Why don't they like cats? The cats never did anything to them.

Without taking his eyes off of Turnip, the vet says in a whisper, I hear you. It's frustrating when people don't like something for no reason, huh? It's a miracle that this cat has made it this far.

Sei's face falls.

The vet places Turnip back inside the trap. Kami pushes her face toward Turnip. She presses a paw against the trap and lets out a quiet meow. It looks like she is trying to calm Turnip. Turnip does not respond. Do the cats know what is happening? Can they guess what they're doing here? Kami looks around the vet's desk and shows interest in his mouse, pen, and stethoscope. When Sei extends her hand, Kami rubs against it fondly. If Sei opened her arms, Kami might jump into her embrace.

We won't know until I do some tests, but it looks like the infection in the mouth is pretty serious. But we can't operate right away. He's very weak right now. Pushing him might be harmful.

The vet reaches toward Turnip's face. His gloved hand coaxes Turnip's mouth open, revealing bloody gums. Turnip does not fight him. He only blinks slowly, completely resigned.

So, does that mean Turnip can't get his operation? Sei asks.

Haesoo waits for the vet's answer, still trying to decide if she should send Sei out of the exam room or let her stay.

Let's keep him here for now and think about it once he's recovered a bit. Did you look after them both? You did a really good job. Are you and your mom going to take him home once he's fixed up?

Auntie is not my mom. Auntie is just a friend. And I'm going to take Turnip home when he's better. So, if Turnip gets an operation, will he get better?

There is a faint tremble in Sei's voice. Haesoo fights back the urge to wrap her arms around the child. If she does, Sei will certainly burst into tears. The weary cat in the trap will hear the child's crying. The sound will intensify its anxiety and fear. Haesoo is surprised at her own thoughts. She does not recognize this person who thinks that a non-human animal has premonitions akin to feelings.

We'll keep him here for now and see how he does. What would you like to do with the other one? If you want to take her home with you, I can run a few basic tests first. If you want to leave her here, we'll run the tests later and let you know what we find.

Haesoo answers, We'll leave Kami here with Turnip. I think that'll be best.

Dear Ms. Euna Noh,

Hello, I'm Haesoo Lim.

I got in touch with you a few times through my lawyer Kyungjin Choi. I believe you remember me. It's been a while— I imagine you're surprised to hear from me.

You might think that this is a rude request, but I'm writing in the hopes of meeting with you.

I've thought it over for a long time before writing to you, and I still think it's only right that I speak with you in person. I wouldn't blame you if you're suspicious of my intentions. You might even think that I have some nerve asking this of you. But I have no other intentions or purpose in mind.

There is something I must say to you in person. I know you're busy, but I hope you could spare just a moment.

To be honest, when the incident first happened, my lawyer

Haesoo watches a movie.

The movie begins with this scene: a middle-aged woman is loading a van. In the van, there aren't any large items like a refrigerator, table, or bed that would take several people to move, but small cardboard boxes. Flashes of small country houses and snowy fields appear in the background. It's the middle of winter. A world taken over by cold. White huffs of breath escape from the woman's mouth as she lugs the boxes to the van. The woman's red, frozen earlobes poke out from under a wool hat.

Are you leaving now?

The sound of footsteps on the dirt path is followed by the shot of a man walking toward the woman. The man is older than the woman. The woman loads the boxes on the ground up into the van one by one as she nods. The wind blows. A dog bays in the distance. The man silently helps the woman with the boxes. The last box looks heavy enough that they need to lift it together.

Have you decided where you're going? the man asks.

The woman answers, Of course.

They stand facing each other. They look impassively at each other for a moment, then shake hands. A goodbye so clean as to be a letdown. The woman leaves, the man remains.

Scene change.

A crowd has gathered around a bonfire. Their cars are parked far in the distance. They do not have a home. They live in cars loaded up with the bare necessities. When they need money, they work part time. At night, they drive around in search of safe, quiet places to park for the night. They wash themselves in public bathrooms and do laundry in coin-op laundromats. They joke with strangers and share stories about their lives to keep from feeling lonely. They show that this is a practicable way of living.

Brief close-ups of the faces gazing into the fire. The sound of crackling wood, of people talking, of the wind, of birds calling, of a low humming. The woman from the van is silent. She seems deep in thought, in a place where the camera cannot infiltrate, in a time that only exists for her.

The woman's eyes are fixed on the blazing fire. What is she seeing? What is the expression that the middle-aged female actor is trying to convey? Perhaps the actor is gazing at herself?

128

Perhaps, searching in the long life she has led, she has located the precise feeling that the protagonist is now engrossed in?

So maybe this is just like watching a movie for her as well, Haesoo thinks. What is she seeing in the movie, in the protagonist, in herself playing the protagonist? What is she looking for?

Cold, huh? How about some tea? Would you like a cup?

A tall, skinny man offers people hot tea. He pours some tea in the woman's stainless steel cup as well. The camera pulls back slowly and shows the woman from behind. The back of the woman sitting in a small camping chair grows tiny and disappears.

There's this scene as well:

The woman works in a kitchen with a ridiculously small hairnet on her head. The white tiles and stainless steel appliances are so clean they appear cold. The other people in the kitchen move silently but quickly. When the alarm buzzes, someone takes food out of the industrial oven, and others cook meat at the grill where great plumes of smoke rise. The woman is washing an endless stream of dishes pouring into an enormous sink. Her hands move fast in the suds-filled water.

During her break, the woman smokes with other workers by the dumpster.

Isn't that funny? I never imagined this place would have such a large kitchen. Who knew they had such an incredibly stocked walk-in? This place could ride out a war. Let's meet back here if there's a war. We'll have a big barbecue before we die, someone says.

Another responds, I had no idea humans ate so much meat every evening. Damn. And I was one of them.

Self-deprecating jokes are interspersed with bitter, weary laughter. The woman sucks hard on the cigarette. The lit end burns bright red.

Let me tell you one thing I learned. I had no idea how good a cigarette tastes after dishes. Why didn't anyone tell me about this?

The woman can make quips like this. There's no way of knowing who she was before. What life she lived, where and how it began to change. Everything is a mystery. The movie is not interested in these questions. This movie is not about that.

The scene changes, and the woman is driving.

A four-lane road stretches before her in a gentle curve. There is no one else in sight. The woman's van glides down the road. Anything that could be considered scenery has been buried in snow. The almost unnerving white of the snow has swallowed up all other colors.

The van stops in the middle of a vast, unending field.

The woman turns off the engine, reclines her seat, and closes her eyes. It looks like she's taking a break. The day is coming to a close. It's getting dark. The woman sits for a long while before fetching a small lantern from the back of the van. She squats behind the van and pees. Then she begins to walk in big strides.

Glimpses of the area that the light reveals show empty fields. Not a tree in sight. Darkness without height or width. The woman marches on. Like someone looking for something.

Like someone with a destination in mind. There is no hesitation in her steps. When she finally stops, she is standing in the middle of darkness. She stares blankly ahead of her.

The camera stays behind her. It does not show her face. It keeps its rigid focus on the woman. She is hardly moving. All at once, everything that surrounds the woman seems to overpower her. All of it feels too real—the wind, the cold, the sounds, the smells.

Is the woman crying?

The woman is crying. Haesoo is unsure why tears are falling. Unsure why the quiet sobs are growing into wails. There is no narrative in this scene. There is nothing to stir the emotion, no sense of tragedy. There is no dramatic arc. So what could be the reason the woman abandons the strong grip she's had on herself?

It's not the woman watching the movie on her sofa who is crying. She does not cry. It's the woman on the screen who is crying. The woman is someone in a movie she has never met, and can never meet.

Dear Ms. Euna Noh,

Hello, I'm Haesoo Lim.

I reached out to you a few times through my lawyer Kyungjin Choi. I wonder if you remember me. My lawyer relayed to me the last message you sent. That you do not wish to be contacted about this matter ever again.

In spite of your wishes, I'm sorry to be contacting you again.

I would like to speak with you in person. It has been a while since the incident and I understand you can't think well of me. I imagine you are surprised by this unwelcome contact. You will, of course, also wonder if I'm approaching you with an ulterior motive. I have no agenda. If I did, I wouldn't have contacted you directly.

If you give me a time and place convenient for you, I will come to you. I will await your answer. If there is anything you are concerned about

Haesoo stops by the vet's office once a day.

Sometimes twice. Three times at most. The vet's office is a thirty-minute walk from her place, and it takes no more than ten minutes for Haesoo to start sweating. She often forgets to put on sunscreen, and loses sleep on those days because of her allergic rash.

This time she carries a parasol.

How is the rescue? Is he doing better? Maru Mom messages her sometimes, and Haesoo replies that Turnip is doing better and will recover quickly. That's a lie. Turnip is more or less the same.

Turnip sometimes looks much more at home in the square in-patient unit than he did on the street. His soot-covered ashen fur is returning to the original ginger, and the wet snout and cuts are slowly healing. He looks peaceful, even, with the cone around his head as he gets his saline injection.

But looks are looks. Looks don't mean anything here. This is the place where the invisible is brought to light. This is the place where the doom that lies beyond the agreeable surface is diagnosed. Perhaps Sei was right to say that a hospital is not a place that fixes sick animals. It's only a place where the invisible is seen, the inaudible is heard, and the end that no one is willing to say out loud is declared.

Recovery is slow because the cat is quite weak, the vet says. We'll continue with the saline injection and wait a little longer. If we operate in this condition, we can't expect a good outcome. There's anesthesia, and surgery is hard on the body. The physical condition has to be at a certain level. Let's give it a few more days.

There's not much Haesoo can do besides watch Turnip and listen to the doctor's report about Turnip's lack of progress. He offers her a few words of comfort and quickly leaves. Sick animals are always coming through his door.

Haesoo doesn't know how often Sei comes to the vet's office or how long she stays. Haesoo accompanies her on visits when Sei asks her to, and comes alone when she hasn't heard from Sei. She doesn't want to pressure the child. Even so, she sits in the waiting room for a moment after looking in on Turnip and waits.

On Friday afternoon, she runs into Sei outside the vet's office.

Sei hitches up her bag and runs toward her. Auntie! Auntie, I got a new phone!

The child reaches into her pocket and pulls out a phone much bigger than her hand. The wallpaper on the phone's screen shows colorful marbles. No, on closer inspection, they're scoops of ice cream. Behind the ice cream is Sei's hand making a peace sign, and a larger hand behind that. Peach nail polish. It must be Sei's mom.

Really? Can I see? Oh, it looks cool. I'm glad you got a new phone, Sei. You were upset that you broke the old one.

Yes. I'm going to be really, really careful with this one. Because this phone is very expensive.

Sei wipes the screen with her shirt and carefully puts it back in her pocket.

They go into the vet's office together. As soon as they enter, Sei calls Kami. After a few escape attempts from in-patient care, Kami is now allowed to roam the waiting room. The cat seems to get along just fine with the vet's dog, too. Sei gestures at Kami, who comes over and rubs her cheek on Sei's hand. But that's it. Kami's attention instantly shifts to other people, other animals.

Kami seems happy with this strange world bustling with new things.

Auntie, I thought Turnip was a boy and Kami's a girl. What about you?

Turnip is lying quietly behind the glass pane of the in-patient care room. Sei waves, but Turnip doesn't respond.

I don't know. I never thought about it.

Turnip is a girl, and Kami is a boy. What a twist, huh? I thought they were at least one year old, but the vet said they were only ten months old. I was so surprised. Or was it nine? Anyway, they're just babies, right?

Babies. Haesoo smiles. Sei is busy examining Turnip. Which is younger, a ten-year-old child or a ten-month-old cat? Is it appropriate for such children to be in the situations they face? Given what they're going through, aren't these children much more grown-up than Haesoo?

The child waves at Turnip. There's a red scrape on her palm. There's a long scratch on her left elbow, and a dark bruise is printed on her wrist.

What happened to your hand? Did you hurt yourself?

Yeah, I fell down. During practice, says Sei, her expression stiffening.

Haesoo thinks. The children shove Sei against a wall, mocking, yelling, berating, goading. Enjoying the scary beat of the ball passed around the edges as she darts out of the way alone in the court. How Sei must feel surrounded by the sounds of feet, shouts, laughter.

Haesoo wants to tell her that she is not going to let the children get away with being so clearly malicious. She wants to promise Sei that she'll make sure they never treat her that way again. But Haesoo says nothing. She waits. She waits for the child to tell her more. For her to want to tell her more.

Auntie, do you know why I got a new phone? Sei asks as they leave the vet's. One side of her cheek is sticking out where she's sucking on a lollipop.

Because you dropped the old one in the toilet?

No. I was going to just get it fixed, but I got a new phone instead.

Yeah? Hmm.

The preliminary games are starting soon. Next week? No, the week after that! Dodgeball. Mom said she would come. So she got me this phone. To cheer me on.

Yeah?

Didn't you see it, Auntie? There's a really big banner hanging in front of the school.

The skies are beginning to clear. Strong, scorching sunlight beats down. Haesoo takes it as a good sign.

Really? I didn't see it. Remember I promised you last time? To not go to your school anymore?

Sei smiles.

Do you want to win first place? Haesoo asks.

Sei answers, No.

She purses her lips and looks coyly up at Haesoo—it's a secret.

The weather forecast for the start of monsoon season has been inaccurate for weeks.

Monday morning, Haesoo settles down at a table in a restaurant with a view of the entrance. It's a sunny day. She can see the brightly lit street through the window.

Monday morning. The day of the week when one's heart fills with resolve and promise. A good time to forget the failures and mistakes of the previous week and start fresh. Time to light the fires of hope and expectation.

Haesoo has no problem with the fact that she is meeting with Taeju on a Monday morning. They don't need to meet on weekends when the tension loosens and everything skews emotional. They no longer have that kind of relationship. They cannot croon words of comfort or encouragement to each other. Taeju walks through the entryway on the other side of the restaurant.

When did you get here? You're early.

Just now.

They say hello, ignoring the awkwardness. The waitress comes over with menus. Haesoo orders. Drinks are served first, and Taeju pours Haesoo's drink into her glass. They keep themselves busy, determined not to stumble upon an unpleasant stillness.

They talk about the house, about how to divide it. They came to an agreement on this a long time ago, and they have no objections to it now. The problem is timing. They are both aware that they have no choice but to wait. There is no sense in voicing certain suspicions. Kindnesses that have now crossed the line. Generosity that can never be repaid. They have to be careful not to let these things to the surface.

The food is served and the topic changes.

Have you decided what to do about your job at the counseling center? Taeju asks.

Haesoo answers, Not yet.

Taeju stirs his drink with the straw. The ice clinks.

Didn't you say you would discuss it with Lee? I thought you were already back at work.

The center made the decision, and I was informed of it. I did send a request for the paperwork on the decision process. And Jo Minyoung. I'm also going to demand an explanation regarding what she said in the meeting.

Haesoo comes close to cursing. She's suddenly furious about what that traitor Jo Minyoung did to her. She cuts the sandwich in half with a knife. The blade goes through the sandwich and scrapes hysterically at the plate beneath. Taeju gives her a look. Haesoo doesn't care.

You don't have to push that hard. Lee's under pressure as well. You can understand, right? There are other counseling centers in the world. It's not good to keep yourself in this state. It's not good for you.

Is anything good for me anymore?

You can start looking for good things from now on. You can.

What? Where? How? Haesoo swallows these questions. She's not here for generic consolations. She's not here to be reminded that she was once married to this man. This man who now throws insensitive advice at her from a safe distance.

Be realistic. Accept what you need to accept and forget what you should forget. That's how you can start over, whatever you choose to do.

And what did you accept, forget, and start over? But Haesoo swallows these questions as well. She has to take Taeju's words at face value. She wants to twist his words, argue, mock him. She wants to pick a fight.

Everyone goes through rough patches in life. Just tell yourself you're going through one of those. It won't be easy, but you'll gain something. Didn't you use to say this to your clients a lot?

Why is he so chatty today? Her patience crumbles. She asks why he had to put her through this separation during her "rough patch." She does not put it in so many words, but Taeju gets it right away.

Let's not get into that. That's a separate issue. He lowers his voice and draws a line.

Haesoo's voice rises. No. You made it the issue the moment you said it. If you were even the least bit considerate, you would not have ended things now, in this way. You just wanted to get out. You couldn't bear to see how people were gossiping about me, about you. You were sick and tired of explaining to everyone why your wife who always threw around words like *morals* and *decency* made such an asinine mistake. Should I go on?

That has nothing to do with you. They are separate matters. It's not what you think.

Is that so? Then tell me. Don't just say you're "tired" or that this is "too much." Give me the real reason.

Stop it. I'm not here to argue with you.

Can't you please be honest?

Honest? About what?

For once, just say what you're thinking. Let it all out. Or admit I'm right. Are you scared to say the truth out loud? What's there to be afraid of at this point?

I don't know what you want to hear from me, but it's all in the past now. There's no point in dredging things up again.

Taeju steps back and Haesoo advances. The distance between them neither closes nor opens. When the conflict reaches its climax, they will see what lies at the bottom of each other's humanity—a sight they have seen ad nauseam. Violent fury toward each other, scathing accusations, tireless attacks. Do they still have some of it left down there in the bottom?

But Haesoo will not let this go. It isn't just about resentment and blame. Clearly, there's something like pleading and begging in this tenacity.

Don't you think we need to just let it all out in the open and talk, just once? Isn't it ridiculous that we're sitting all dressed up like this on a Monday morning like people at a business meeting, eating sandwiches we don't even like?

Don't even like? I like them. I like sandwiches, Taeju says with a blank expression. You just didn't know what I liked.

This shuts her up. The waitress comes over to fill their glasses. Haesoo and Taeju silently work on their meals. Lettuce, salami, olives. She picks them up and eats them one by one, trying not to say anything.

Taeju's advice is reasonable. There is a reason for his stance. He gets to decide what needs to be done. In the end, she cannot decide that for him. She is aware of this.

Haesoo decides to start the conversation over.

After a long silence, she changes the topic. How are you doing these days? Everything okay?

Taeju is happy to play along. They ask after each other's family with whom they no longer have any relationship. They make small talk. They watch helplessly as the conversation extends in a neat, straight line.

Perhaps the end of their marriage had nothing to do with the incident. Perhaps all the incident did was create a small fracture in their relationship. Maybe this was only the catalyst for all the problems they had ignored.

Oh, I almost forgot. I gathered just the important things. Haesoo hands him a bag just as they are about to finish their meal. Taeju's diaries, photo albums, diplomas, a letter of appointment.

You didn't have to. Thanks anyway. Taeju looks at his watch. He's about to leave.

Come to me for therapy. Some point in the future. If you need help, that is, Haesoo blurts out. Taeju freezes halfway out of his chair and gives her a confused look.

You won't have to tell me all the details. Because I already know you well. That will save time. I won't charge you too much.

Haesoo tries to smile casually.

It goes without saying that Taeju will never come to her for therapy. He is drifting off into an unknown world. If he needs help, he will need help in a place Haesoo does not know about. She will know less and less about Taeju. Their lives will move away from each other, leaving no point of convergence.

Taeju leaves first. He doesn't answer or say much of a good-bye, and walks out of the restaurant alone as if to punish her.

Dear Juhyun,

It's getting hotter these days. How are you?

Remember how I told you I'm out trying to rescue a sick cat? The cat was finally rescued a few days ago. Where I failed miserably, the neighborhood kid succeeded in one go. Isn't it strange? The girl said she nudged the cat into the trap as it walked in on its own, but how is that possible? All of my own attempts failed.

You may already know this, but cats get very violent when they're threatened. Too scary to go near. But the kid pushed it into the trap so easily. I still can't believe it. Maybe the cat wanted to live. Maybe the cat walked into the trap praying we would save it. Maybe that's how it happened.

I go to the vet's office every day to visit the cat. It has made little progress. The vet says he wouldn't be surprised if the cat died right now. Well, he doesn't put it like that, of course. The cat is alive. Sometimes I think it's not just alive, but really struggling to stay alive. Maybe that's why it hasn't died yet.

I don't know why I'm doing this. I don't know if what I did to the cat was "rescue it," or if I'm "helping." If you were here, you would have said that helping oneself is the first step. You might have even said that I'm using the cat as an excuse to avoid my problems.

Juhyun, I reached out to that man's mother. Jeonggi Park's mother. I emailed and texted through the lawyer, but there's no response. I don't think I'll ever hear back from her. Maybe I should have done something that day you and I went to the community center together—introduce myself, say hello, say something?

But how could I have said something to her? I was in no way prepared. What would I have said? What could be said that would make

The eyes are the most striking features of Turnip's face.

When Turnip opens her eyes, the blue-green irises surrounding the dark pupils become clear. Her eyes look like glass marbles, like twinkling planets. The yellow fur in the shape of an opera mask around her eyes makes her look silly, and the large spot on her nose gives her a grumpy look.

Turnip, how are you today?

Unlike most days, when Haesoo finds Turnip lying exhausted, today she's sitting and looking up at Haesoo. She licks her front paws and scratches her ear with her back foot. Haesoo sees the chapped corners of Turnip's mouth when she yawns. The excruciating pain that once plagued her seems to have retreated.

She presses her forehead against the glass pane of the in-patient unit and meets Turnip's eye. Turnip blinks slowly. Indirect, but clearly an amiable gesture. Haesoo works up the courage to put her index finger through the hole in the pane. Turnip isn't frightened. She comes closer, sniffs, and touches her nose to it. Does Turnip know? Does she know why Haesoo brought her here? Does she finally understand?

Haesoo sometimes forgets that Turnip is just an animal. Or rather, Haesoo cannot help but think that when people say "animal," the meaning it covers is so shallow and limiting. The wordless connection between her and Turnip gives her a strange sense of safety. It's the sort of feeling she could not imagine in a world clamorous with unending words.

Understanding and empathy. Sympathy and acceptance.

Are they possible only in such complete silence?

Haesoo has never feared words. She believed she had a thorough understanding of them. She believed she interpreted, explained, argued, agreed, confessed, and through them expressed the invisible inner self with precision. She was confident she was able to see everyone this way, see into them and through them at the same time.

Haesoo knows now that she was just a person in a flood of words who wasted her own words on things that did not need articulating. She sees that she has never once imagined where her words are born, how they live, and where they die.

Hi, the vet says. Turnip's doing okay today, isn't she? She gets a little better and then a little worse from day to day. Let's watch her for another couple of days before we make a decision. Sometimes they do take a sudden turn for the worse. The vet gives her a nod and walks off to the exam rooms.

Haesoo stays there a little longer. All nine slots of the in-patient care unit are full. Two cats, and the rest are dogs. The calico next door to Turnip is wearing a red collar. On a thumbnail-sized pendant is the name "Singo".

Haesoo takes her time looking at the animals.

The Maltese in diapers barks endlessly, and the pug is panting and coughing. The poodle is nodding off, using his chew bone as a pillow. They wag their tails hello when Haesoo waves. Some of them stick out their tongues and spin in place with excitement they can't hide.

As far as Haesoo can see, none of the animals are in as serious a condition as Turnip. At least they have owners. They have homes to return to when they're better. Haesoo looks back at Turnip as she leaves the in-patient care room. Turnip is limp on the floor again. Haesoo waves to no response.

It rains for a few days.

It seems that the forecast, which predicted it would be the driest monsoon season in history, was wrong. The rain starts and stops as if to mock the weather forecast that changes by the hour.

The next day, Haesoo goes to the supermarket. The store is packed with people trying to get out of the heat. She browses the electronics and furniture section of the third floor, then goes down to the second floor where the groceries and beauty products are. The sports equipment and pet supply sections are in the basement.

Haesoo picks out a pair of blue knee and elbow protectors. She also grabs a set of purple hair bands. Then she heads straight to the pet section. Pet food of all sizes, colorful packaging, treats of all ingredients and tastes, equipment of indecipherable use, and adorable little toys fill the aisle.

Let me know if I can help you with anything, the sales person organizing the shelves says.

Haesoo browses the toys. There are poles like fishing rods with feathers, plush fish, jingling balls, and soft cushions. Excuse me, she says. If I get one of these, do they play with it on their own?

The sales person looks up from stocking the bottom shelf. Dog or cat?

Cat.

Is this your first time shopping for cat toys?

Yes.

The sales person gets up and removes her gloves. Then she offers a brief introduction to the items bearing the "top seller" tags. Haesoo learns that cats' toy preferences are dependent on age, personality, and tastes. At this point, she isn't sure if she will ever find out what Turnip's tastes are by giving her these toys. Turnip may not have enough time left.

Having pets is just like having children, the sales person says. They require so much attention and energy. Do you have a cat?

Haesoo says yes and picks out a few more toys. A fishing rod with a red feather, a spongy ball with a bell inside, and a plush fish. It costs less than 10,000 won all together.

If you keep the tag on, you can return the items, the sales person says in a hushed voice. Haesoo looks back at her. The woman adds, You can exchange them, too, of course.

Through the narrow, crowded marketplace is the convenience store and stationery store, and a wall with flower and tree murals. Beyond is a different world. The noise and stench that surround the shopping area turn into something entirely different.

Sei's school is not far from here.

Excitement and Fun! Dodgeball Tournament!

Haesoo spots the large banner hanging at the school gate just as Sei said she would. *Learning fountain of love and wisdom.* Other banners read, *This is a no-parking zone. A safe school zone protects children. School Bullying Prevention Day. Report School Bullying Now*, says another banner in red.

May I help you? a security guard asks. Like others around her, she tells him she is here for the dodgeball tournament. The guard nods her in. He must think she is a parent. She settles down in the bleachers with other people who look like parents. They're under a large zelkova tree in a corner of the schoolyard.

There are fewer than ten adults watching the game. Maybe because this is only the preliminaries. There is no excitement on the field, either. Parents call their child's name, wave, and take pictures. Some hold handmade signs and balloon sticks. A few of them spot the homeroom teacher and sidle up to say hello.

Haesoo stays where she is, unsure of what to do. This does not seem like the right moment to pass Sei the protective gear, headband, and beverage she bought. She has no idea how the child might react if she says hello. Or how it might affect the game. Haesoo chooses to wait.

Today's games take place not on the dirt athletic field but on the green grass. The grass court was off-limits when the children were practicing together. Striking white lines have been painted on the grass. The whistle blows. The players run down from the bleachers. The rest of the children applaud and cheer. It is a bright, lively noise.

The tangle of blue and yellow uniforms quickly separate by color. Haesoo searches among the yellow shirts with Fourth Grade, Class Two printed on them.

She catches glimpses of Sei among the children busily moving about. She takes a few steps closer but does not look in Haesoo's direction. She does not look in the direction of the cheering children in the bleachers, either. She keeps her eyes focused on where she stands.

The game begins.

Truth be told, one could hardly call this a game. To Haesoo, this is child's play. There is no expert knowledge, sophisticated technique, or strategy. The children dash around the court in a herd as the ball flies back and forth. They shrink when the ball flies from the other side, and strut when their side gets hold of the ball. This is not a place for skill or talent. The movement of the ball is sudden, impulsive, and entirely guided by luck.

The white whizzing ball takes the children out one by one. The adults in attendance let out soft groans. The players who are hit move to the back line on the other side and help with the defense. As the number of players remaining on the court dwindles, the cheering grows more intense. The children in the bleachers shout their friends' names, clap, and hoot.

Haesoo's mind wanders.

Having a life. Making a living. Work. Therapy. She has to start working. For the past year, she has lived on severance, unemployment, and savings. Is one year a long time to go without work? Or is it much too short? Whatever the answer, she knows that she has reached a limit. And not just financially. She is no longer interested in watching herself turn into an indistinct recluse.

She can't keep living like this.

Are you here to cheer for your kid? the woman standing next to Haesoo asks.

Which class? the woman asks. My kid is in Class Five.

Class Two.

Oh, I hear there are many good players in Class Two. My kid has never beat them in the practice games. Looks like his class is going to lose again today, huh?

Haesoo smiles softly instead of an answer.

There are about five children left on the court. The teacher playing referee blows the whistle and stops the game for a moment. Then she gathers the children and says something. It looks like she is giving them a warning. The teacher points at Sei and another kid and says something to them specifically. The two children are looking away from each other, hanging their heads in silence.

Is that Sori? The popular girl who picks on Sei? But the truth can't be that simple.

Sei's truth and Sori's truth must be standing opposite each other, sharpening their knives.

The game resumes. The ball starts to fly around again. The boisterous atmosphere is revived. The line between my side and your side, our team and your team becomes impermeable, and everyone is focused on winning. The children in the game and the children cheering from the bleachers both do their best not to lose.

From a distance, this all looks very innocent and somewhat desperate. Perhaps this is the nature of all games. Sides are formed, attacks are launched, and victory is contingent upon taking down the other side—this must be the fundamental nature of sports. Do children organically experience moments of savage single-minded focus in the heat and excitement of the game?

Sei loses her balance and stumbles a few times. Haesoo's heart drops. But still Sei ducks and jumps out of the way in nimble, deft movements. She is one of three children remaining on the court. And finally, she catches the ball. There is only one person remaining on the other side. Sei holds up the ball with both hands and cautiously steps up close to the center line. She is incredibly nervous.

This is the final move that could end this game. The shot at victory.

But Sei drops the ball for no apparent reason. The ball slips out of her hands and rolls into the other side's court. The player on the other side quickly snatches up the ball and hurls it right away. Sei, still standing by the center line in a daze, is hit on the right shoulder.

∽

Dear Euna Noh,

Hello. It's Haesoo Lim.

I have reached out to you a few times through my lawyer Kyungjin Choi. I am writing to you because there's something I would like to say to you in person. I would be grateful if you could give me just a little bit of your time.

I know that you declined any further contact regarding this matter. I am not trying to find out something. And it isn't my goal to discuss or negotiate anything with you. And, of course, I am not asking for a favor. All I want is to tell you my side of the story.

What I said on the show was inappropriate. But I didn't say it out of ill-will. Until I received my script that day, I didn't know about the controversy. When I first got my script, I didn't think much of it. At the time,

∽

On Wednesday afternoon, Haesoo leaves the house.

One hour by car. But she takes public transportation instead of driving. She makes the decision with the trip back home in mind. She may not return feeling the same way she did when she left. She will most definitely be a little worn down, battered. She has to get herself home. She can't anticipate how heavy and broken her heart will be.

She walks to the subway station. When she arrives at her stop, she takes the bus from the station. She does not hurry. Her steps are unagitated, almost leisurely.

She arrives at a café in a residential area. No signs or bright lights outside. The café looks like an average house. But through the gate is a vast front yard and several wooden tables. The yard is more of a garden—a beautifully kept flowerbed and lush shrubbery catch Haesoo's eye.

Haesoo goes inside and settles at a table by the window. The café is full of large potted plants, the air is thick with the smell of grass, and the tree growing through the roof in the middle of the room creates a grounded, grand atmosphere.

The person Haesoo is waiting for arrives exactly on time. Euna Noh. Wife of Jeonggi Park. She arrives just as Haesoo finishes the last of the coffee in her cup.

Are you Ms. Haesoo Lim? she asks. Shoulders back, back straight, the woman looks taller than she is. She doesn't even look her age. That might be the bright tone of her jacket working to her benefit.

Hello. Nice to meet you.

Haesoo springs from her seat and greets her. The woman puts down her bag, beckons the wait staff, and sits down across from Haesoo. Not too far, not too close, this is the right distance for the careful study of a person's face. Haesoo holds her gaze. Nothing seems excessive. The eyebrow shape, skin tone, shade of lipstick. Everything is natural. A faint scent of citrus wafts up each time she moves.

The two women look slightly away from each other. A new cup of coffee is served. The woman takes a sip and meets Haesoo's eye again as if to say that she is ready now.

Thank you for meeting with me.

So, says the woman. You had something you wanted to say?

There is no expression on the woman's face to speak of. There is no kindness, no hostility.

Haesoo sees no sadness or anger in her. This throws her off.

First, I wanted to offer you a belated apology. I never imagined that something I said could lead to something like this.

The woman rubs the handle of her teacup with her fingers. The cup clacks against the saucer. Haesoo fights the urge to stop talking. She does not intend to bypass this process by simply saying she's sorry. If "sorry" was all she wanted to say, she would not have begged to meet with her, in person no less.

Haesoo must tell her.

From within herself, she must find the words she can say and the words she must say. With patience, she must pull them up from deep below, one at a time, in their order.

I'll be frank. Honestly, I didn't know much about Mr. Park at the time. I didn't know what he looked like, his age, or even the fact that he was an actor. I found out just before the show when I received the script. I didn't know about the issues surrounding him, either. If I had known something, even a little bit, I wouldn't have read my lines so flippantly.

The woman looks straight at Haesoo. Did she say something wrong? Did she blurt out something she should not have? She cannot read the emotion in the woman's eyes.

So what have you learned since? About Jeonggi Park? the woman asks.

All Haesoo really knows is that he was an actor. The woman waits for her answer. Haesoo haltingly lists the shows and films he was featured in. *Brave Guys*, *Ode to Autumn*, *Sunset Hill*. Among them are titles whose meanings she can't figure out, like *Murachi* and *Hongmi*.

What did you think?

Excuse me?

You saw Jeonggi Park as an actor. What did you think of him as an actor? I'm just curious. What do therapists think when they watch these shows?

The conversation has turned. The woman takes the reins. Is she trying to test Haesoo? Is she trying to see if she'll take the bait? Haesoo is more than happy to oblige her.

I wondered what he would have been like in bigger roles. I got the sense that his roles were generally small.

Weren't they? Why didn't they give him bigger roles, these directors? Strange, isn't it? Honestly, there were a few good opportunities that came his way, but something didn't work out each time. The bigger the anticipation, the worse they fell apart.

The woman's eyes are fixed on the table.

The One Song. I liked him in that, Haesoo suddenly blurts out. The number of scenes in which he appeared in the movie could be counted on one hand. Still, the scene where he stood alone in a snowy field stayed with her for a long time. Dressed in a comically large jacket, shivering all over, as he watched the van drive away from him. She can recall the look in his eyes.

Yes, that movie. That was a good role. He didn't agree, but that character was most like him. You know how there are people whose plans always get screwed up at a crucial moment? I might even say that his life was distilled into that role. That made the movie kind of unnerving, too.

There is a pause in the conversation. The conversation might have lost its way. A dog barks. Outside the window a white dog prances across the garden.

The woman says, He and I had filed for divorce at the time. Strictly speaking, he and I have no legal ties now. If his mother was here instead of me, she would take a very different tone.

I'm sorry.

I heard that you reached out to her a few times. Did it occur to you that you were too late?

I should have met with her sooner and apologized. I'm sorry. Haesoo bows her head.

I'm sure you heard through your lawyer that we planned to sue at the time? That was me. I was going to sue for defamation of the reputation of the deceased, and everything else we can sue for. But Jeonggi's mother said that her son wasn't the kind of person to kill himself over some uninformed people's ignorant comments. He wouldn't have made that choice over a few words.

The woman looks at Haesoo. In the moment, Haesoo loses her grip on the sequence of thoughts she was drawing up. Silence enfolds her. She snaps out of it and earnestly apologizes again.

Do you have anything else you'd like to say besides "sorry"? the woman asks.

Does she have anything else she'd like to say? Is there something that she must say? She confesses that she regrets having spoken thoughtlessly about someone she did not know. She confesses that she is racked with guilt over the tragedy and sorrow that her words brought on. She says she has been atoning deeply for her actions.

Atoning? How? the woman asks.

What am I doing to show regret?

In that moment, Haesoo thinks of words like *compensation* and *reparation*. A clear way to demonstrate a sentiment that cannot be seen. Placing the final period at the end of an argument. It had occurred to Haesoo that things might come to this. She uses indirect and oblique terms to figure out what she means.

You are missing the point, the woman says. She takes a sip of coffee and says, I sometimes wonder if everyone these days is just nuts about atoning. Everywhere you go, someone is always browbeating someone else to atone. Atone. Why aren't you showing remorse? Are you sincerely atoning? It's pretty annoying. But when you think about it, isn't "atoning" for the benefit of the person who did wrong? I imagine no one would want to make the same mistake twice. Aren't you old enough to know that life isn't long enough for repeating mistakes?

He was not a good husband, the woman goes on. But he was a good actor and a good son. He was in a bind in many ways at the time. You don't need to know the details of it, but his mother is right. He wasn't the kind of person to make such a decision because of a few comments from people who don't know better. That's why his mother didn't think she needed your apology.

What kind of person was Jeonggi Park? Haesoo wonders. When she read about this man getting into fights with fellow actors, destroying film sets, having footage of such moments released on the internet, being exposed by detailed eyewitness accounts and victims coming forward in the news, she thought she knew everything about him. That class of person. That kind of man. Staggering through life like a drunk, turning life itself into mayhem. But what she saw in the movies and shows was not so one-dimensional. And by the woman's account, Jeonggi was becoming less and less recognizable. She begins to see the inner life of a person she cannot completely fathom.

Haesoo sits up straight.

Don't get me wrong, the woman says. I'm not saying this to alleviate your feelings of guilt. I'm not saying you didn't do anything wrong. A look of disdain emerges on the woman's face. The hate and resentment hidden under the calm veneer is starting to show. Or maybe that's just Haesoo's imagination. People burst into laughter at the table across the aisle. They take turns calling each other's name and teasing each other.

I'm sure you took a hit, too. You must feel wrongly accused and want to clear your name. Your stance, your position. That's all people ever want. I don't think that's atoning. Isn't shutting up closer to atoning? What's the use of saying anything this late? Shouldn't you be left with your share of the burden to bear?

The woman has no intention of hearing Haesoo out. She didn't come out here to listen. Everything Haesoo says is an excuse. There is nothing she could say that would be more valuable than silence.

Haesoo resists the urge to release the words sunk down deep inside her. Things she could not say, things she must not say—Haesoo accepts the fact that these are strictly her share. They are hers to bear. They should not be discussed or shared with others. Just as Jeonggi Park had, just as this woman sitting across from her is doing, she must shut up about things that cannot be articulated. And so comes the gutting understanding of "atonement," which she only knew on the level of vocabulary.

Yes. I understand what you mean, Haesoo answers.

The woman grabs her bag, gets up, and leaves the café. Haesoo's eyes follow the woman as she makes her way through the garden out front.

Suddenly, Haesoo remembers this: *Indignity? What's the big deal with indignity? You can't throw a rock out in the street without hitting something undignified. Indignity is all around, huh?*

Voice full of anger. Derisive smile. Haesoo once heard this line in a movie. It was Jeonggi Park's character. And the movie ended up being his last. Because of her. Because of something she had spouted. Or maybe it was for a reason she will never know. Or maybe there was no reason to begin with. Whatever it is, she will never know. She will never know, so there isn't anything left for her to say.

Dear Euna Noh,

I spoke on the show.

I said that it was irresponsible of Jeonggi Park to fight with his fellow actors and make a mess of the film set. And that because he did not see what he had done wrong, his fellow actors were testifying against him and exposing him in droves. Lack of talent, bad temper, defaulting on his financial obligations—there was a reason for these negative opinions of him. I said that he had brought all of it upon himself and that he needed to take responsibility for it. That even if he was certifiably psychologically unstable, people may not empathize with him.

To be honest, I did not know about the incidents. I learned about them for the first time that morning, when I read through the script in the green room. Nonetheless, I said exactly what was written. Without a thought in my head, as if I knew everything

She dwells there for a moment. In her mind, she scraps all the letters she has written to Euna Noh. Precise vocabulary, clear sentences—she disposes of the hope that these things can convey a message. As she rips up the letter, she throws these words down into a deep, dark silence in herself where they will never be found again.

Then Haesoo gets up and leaves the café.

Haesoo takes the packed bus and train home.

As she opens the gate and steps into her yard, the precarious balance inside her tips over. Strength drains and tension releases. It feels as though she is leaking and flowing out of herself. She focuses on the chill that sweeps over her.

It's a hot, stuffy day.

She opens all the windows in her house and sits on the sofa. Her eyes slowly move from this part of the house to that.

The living room cabinet and television. The wallpaper without patterns. The small coffee table. Everything is the same. Nevertheless, she cannot shake the feeling that something has changed. The sensation lingers.

Somewhere in the distance the sound of cicadas comes in waves, advancing and receding. Everything feels surreal. Is she performing a role like an actor right now? If so, what is the role she's playing? What is the character she is supposed to play? A villain who has done something unforgivable? A perpetrator who cannot be forgiven? Or maybe the victim of a harsh accusation. A loser defeated by hardship. A moron who lost herself in the throes of anguish.

She turns the radio on low, goes into the kitchen, and opens the refrigerator.

From the produce drawer, she removes a shriveled apple and orange, the tomatoes and mushrooms that have gone soft. She takes out the containers of leftovers, the contents of which she no longer remembers. She removes the bottles of condiments and sauces that have expired and throws out the unopened meal packages. The refrigerator bursting with rotting things begins to clear up.

The freezer is in much worse shape. Sweat pouring, Haesoo opens the packaging, looks at the frozen contents, and tosses them into a large garbage bag. She is amazed by the accumulation of unidentifiable foodstuffs so deep inside the freezer. She cannot remember when and where she purchased them. She had no idea how much of it there really was.

She tries to focus on the simple act of cleaning. Sorting, finding, checking, and throwing away brings her something of a comfort. Or perhaps it's closer to a lesson. Or maybe it's just a self-imposed metaphor of what must be done: keep what needs to be kept, throw away what needs to be thrown out, and fill the empty space with new things.

She has almost finished cleaning out the refrigerator when she gets a call.

Trusty Animal Clinic. Is this Turnip's guardian?

She recognizes the voice of the nurse from the vet's office. A woman who can approach large dogs and wild cats without fear, who deftly assists the vet and has a handle on scheduling. She tells Haesoo that the cat is doing better. The basic tests have been completed, and they might be able to do the surgery next week if she can maintain this condition.

I was going to swing by the clinic this evening, Haesoo says.

Can you come now? The doctor has surgeries scheduled back-to-back for the rest of the day. Would you like to come by and discuss surgery options with him?

The nurse nearly yells the last sentence over barking dogs. Haesoo agrees and heads out.

Darkness begins to fall over the dusky streets. The vet's office is quiet. Kami is asleep on a chair by the window with his belly half-exposed. Haesoo enters quietly so as not to wake the cat. She says hello to the receptionist and goes straight up to the second floor where Turnip's in-patient care room is. The light is on in the exam room.

Through the window on the door, Haesoo can see the vet sleeping with his head down on the desk. The nurse knocks, and he jumps up and waves them in.

You got here quickly. Have a seat.

The vet clicks his mouse and swings the monitor around so she can see Turnip's chart. He opens his eyes wide as if to chase sleep away, and gives her the details. Complete blood count, acute infection, heartworm. Parvo, outer ear infection. Positive, negative, carrier, antibodies. The vet says words that aren't familiar to her. She listens closely.

There's a fluff of yellow animal fur stuck to the top of the vet's eyeglass frame. Each time the vet moves his head, the fur perks up as though it's going to fall off, then softly sags again.

Do you have any questions? the vet asks.

Haesoo asks, Will surgery really make her better? Is this treatable?

Of course. I won't know for sure until I put her under and get a good look inside her mouth, but I think extracting a few teeth should do it. Her white cell count has gone down, and the inflammation has cleared up quite a bit. With continued post-op treatment she'll be all better. I'm a little concerned about how small she is, but she started trying to eat on her own yesterday. If they have a will, they recover quickly.

The vet looks down at the desk calendar crowded with surgery and exam appointments. He suggests next Tuesday for surgery. Haesoo nods.

Oh, about Kami, he says. There's someone who would like to adopt him. She's a regular at our hospital, and she says Kami is so adorable she would like to take him home if it's okay with you. What do you think?

Kami?

She has a Labrador retriever over ten years old. She can be trusted. I'm assuming you're not going to release Kami back onto the street. And we can't keep him here at the clinic. Were you planning on keeping him yourself?

Is it okay if I get back to you after discussing it with Sei?

Oh, the little girl? I hear she came by last Saturday with an armful of treats for Turnip, and our nurse told her that the cat couldn't have any. Please let her know that Turnip is all better now and that she can feed her all she wants.

Haesoo thanks the vet and leaves the exam room. Then she pays Turnip a visit. It seems Turnip has recovered her energy quite a bit overnight. When Turnip sees Haesoo, she meows quietly. Haesoo sticks her finger through the air hole. The cat touches her with her nose and even lightly rubs her finger with her cheek. Her tiny pink nose is moist.

The nurse, who is cleaning the empty unit next to Turnip's, whispers, You can pet her. She's allowing it now.

Really?

Haesoo hesitates. The nurse comes over, opens Turnip's door, and pets Turnip to demonstrate. Haesoo reaches out as well. Turnip does not fight her. She only closes her eyes as though scared, and flinches. The cat is warm and soft.

Why does she suddenly allow people to touch her? Haesoo wonders. She is scared that the sudden change might be a sign of an unforeseen outcome.

But in the moment, Haesoo is profoundly moved. Grateful, relieved, elated. These feelings momentarily light up the darkness inside her.

Was this cat in that unit discharged? Haesoo asks, petting Turnip with one hand. The nurse is spraying down every corner of the little box with a strong-smelling disinfectant.

It would have been a risky operation, so she was discharged yesterday, the nurse answers.

Haesoo doesn't want to know the details. Some stories might have a negative impact on how things work out. With Turnip, with Haesoo, and maybe with Sei as well. This might be an overreaction and a baseless fear.

Can Turnip be discharged right after surgery? Haesoo asks.

The nurse answers, I'll have to ask the doctor, but I think you'll be able to take her home. I wouldn't worry too much.

$\sim$

The heat wave lingers for days.

Punishing sunlight suffocates, then comes a thunderstorm. Rain clouds flock over only to suddenly disperse. Unlike the weather, Haesoo becomes cooler and calmer inside. The things that used to bubble up without warning and make her anxious seem to be receding at last. Words deep inside her must be losing their intensity, struggling, and slowly dying.

On Saturday morning she goes to the vet's office. She has an appointment with Kami's new family. Sei, who has arrived before her, greets her at the door.

Auntie! I gave Turnip some Churu just now and she ate it. She doesn't squirm anymore when I pet her. She doesn't shake her head. Did you know that?

Is that right?

She's so small. I can feel her bones. She's so skinny.

Sei looks tan and healthy. Haesoo locks eyes with Sei, who seems to have grown another inch since a few days ago, and nods in agreement. Sitting in the waiting room, they say goodbye to Kami. The new family arrives exactly on time. They look like mother and daughter. When the door opens, the little girl comes in with a mint-colored carrier slung over one shoulder, followed by a woman with a large paper bag.

Kami! Hey, Kami. How are you?

Kami leaves Sei's side and runs over to the two newcomers. Sei seems crushed.

Cats don't usually like people, but Kami is so friendly. He was so adorable I just had to ask the doctor about adoption. I didn't think you would say yes. Thank you. I was going to come by myself, but my daughter insisted, so here we are. She saw Kami at the hospital a few times. Say hello, Min.

Hello, I'm Min Kim.

Haesoo was right. They are a family. The mother is soft-spoken and speaks kindly. The little girl sitting next to her seems like a happy kid. They must be good people, as the doctor says. They can, at the very least, be trusted not to yell at the cat for no reason, throw trash at him, or threaten him. But is that enough? If it isn't enough, what more do you need and how much of it? And is that something one can verify in the waiting room of a vet's office?

I hear you have a dog. Do you think a cat and a dog will be okay together?

Oh, you don't have to worry about that. We've fostered a few cats before. There weren't any problems. Our Pooh is a gentle dog. He sleeps most of the time now that he's old.

So there are three of you living together?

Four. Me, my husband, Min, and my mother-in-law. The pets will almost never be home by themselves, so not to worry.

If you don't mind, can I ask you a few more questions? Haesoo says. There are a few things I'm worried about.

Of course, please do.

Kami settles down next to Min. It's as if he is expressing his wish to be a member of their family. As Maru Mom advised, Haesoo asks a few more questions. Do you have the consent of all family members? How much do you know about cat behavior? Do you have the means to provide treatment if Kami were to fall ill? Among these are more sensitive questions such as occupation, address, and type of housing.

This is an absurd line of questioning, of course. How rude to demand census information from a perfect stranger by asking intrusive questions. Besides, Haesoo does not know enough about the lives and habits of cats to know what questions to ask. This family might be experts at animal care compared to Haesoo.

But the mother gives thoughtful answers to every question without seeming uneasy.

Would you like to sign a contract? If that would give you peace of mind, I'd be more than happy to, she even says obligingly.

Instead, Haesoo asks her to send news of Kami once in a while.

Sei, is there anything you would like to say?

Looking down at the mint-colored pet carrier, Sei is silent. Haesoo wraps her arm around Sei's shoulder and whispers, It's okay. You can ask her if you have a request.

Sei opens her mouth as though she's about to say something, then shakes her head. That is the end of the adoption process. When the daughter opens the pet carrier door, Kami steps right in.

Kami, are you rushing off without saying goodbye? Take good care of yourself. Be well. Haesoo says all of this in a cheerful voice. But her sadness cannot be completely concealed. The same goes for Sei.

By the way, we brought some treats. I heard that the cat who was rescued with Kami is still at the clinic. Min and I will pray for a speedy recovery. Oh, and we also brought some *yakgwa* cookies. We bought them at the rice cake place near our house. They're delicious and not too sweet.

The mother offers a yellow paper bag. Sei takes it. Inside the bag are cans of food and Churu, and two pretty boxes of cookies. The mother and daughter say goodbye. This time, the mother leads the way with the pet carrier. The daughter follows. They slowly make their way to the crosswalk.

Haesoo and Sei stand side by side and watch as they leave.

Should we go say hi to Turnip?

As Haesoo turns to Sei, she bursts out of the clinic. Haesoo runs after her, but the kid is too fast. She zips across the road as the green light flashes, catching up with the mother and daughter. The light changes. Haesoo has to stand at the crosswalk and watch from across the street.

Through the constant stream of cars, Haesoo catches brief glimpses of Sei. The three of them are standing together talking. Or rather, it seems Sei is doing the talking. Sei passes something to Min.

The light changes again. Sei runs back across the street as she did the first time.

You have to be careful when you cross the street, Haesoo says. You know that, right? When the green light is flashing you're supposed to wait for the—

Before she can finish her sentence, the child falls into her arms. She is out of breath, her shoulders dramatically rising and dropping. Is she sobbing? Should Haesoo tell her this is not goodbye forever? Tell her she can always ask after him? That she can go see him if she wants? Console her with promises she can't keep? But when the child looks up, there

169

is no sign of tears. Sei seems more sure than Haesoo has ever seen her.

What did you say? Haesoo asks.

I gave them a note. I wrote it yesterday.

A note? You wrote them a letter?

No. It's not a letter. It's a list of three promises I wanted them to keep.

Three?

The child bites her lip nervously, deciding if she wants to share. Then she answers: Make Kami his own room. Say good night before he goes to sleep. Let him eat all the treats he wants once a month. Sei must want these things for herself, not so much for Kami. Haesoo sees this, of course.

Very good. Well done. That's terrific, Haesoo says as she pats Sei on the head. They walk back to the clinic to check on Turnip, who is about to go into surgery. The vet gives them a brief description of the procedure. With nothing left to do but wait, Haesoo and Sei prepare to leave.

Haesoo gives Sei the gifts she bought at the supermarket. While Sei checks out the elbow and knee protectors and the purple headbands, she looks up at Haesoo once in a while.

Auntie, she calls on the way out. You can come see me at my school next week. If you're bored. To see me play.

Are the dodgeball games still going on? I thought they were almost over.

Oh, the games get canceled when it's raining or too hot. So they keep getting postponed.

So when's the game?

The semifinals are next Friday. At four.

Next Friday at four? Okay. I'll be there. Do you like your presents? If you don't like them, we can go to the store and exchange them.

Um, can I be honest?

Haesoo nods. Sei stalls for a moment. Then she flashes a wicked smile. Honestly, I really like it. I love purple. It's pretty.

Haesoo and Sei walk down the main street together and turn into the alley. Sometimes the child looks up at her with an unspeakably affectionate expression. What does one call this? Friendship, understanding, camaraderie? A certain closeness that cannot be put to words has been etched in Haesoo's heart as well.

Did the series of events she experienced with the child change Haesoo? Did spending this season with Sei affect Haesoo's daily life in some way? Years from now, how will Sei remember this period in her life? What did Haesoo and Sei give and receive between them?

Auntie, have you been to the ginkgo tree lot since we rescued Turnip? the child asks when they reach the crossroads. A dog barks in the distance.

No, I haven't. Have you been there?

Three baby kittens appeared. Maru Mom told me the other day. She said they are really little babies. She said they're really, really cute.

Really?

Do you wanna go see them next time? Let's give them the cat food we got today.

Okay. Let's do it.

∽

It happened so suddenly, in a place no one was paying attention to.

No, that isn't the right way to put it. Nothing is coincidental. Nothing is out of the blue. So what long chain of cause and effect has led to this incident? If one thinks of every event as a reaction to something else, does that make it easier to swallow?

On Friday afternoon, Haesoo finds a seat under the awning among the other families who have come to watch the game.

It's a sweltering day. The sun beats through the fabric of the awning. But the parents don't care. Pouring sweat or not, they move busily to find better seats with a better view of their children. Some people cheer loudly or call their children's names. Haesoo feels removed from the excitement.

When the match between Class One and Class Seven ends, the Class Two and Class Six players come down to the court. Sei is toward the back of the procession. She is wearing her new knee and elbow protectors. Her hair is held back neatly by the headband.

Teams, line up!

The teacher serving as the referee gets their attention.

The children quickly move onto the court. The two teams each huddle on their sides, do their cheer, and stand in a row. A ritual for affirming resolve. Performing unity. The children wear a serious look.

The referee blows the whistle. The ball is tossed high in the air, and the children at the center line jump high. Class Seven gets the ball. The attack begins.

It's really hot out today, says someone standing next to Haesoo. Are you here to watch the game? Which team are you rooting for?

She seems a few years younger than Haesoo. When she says she's rooting for Class Two, she lights up.

The woman takes half a step closer and adds in a whisper, They have some big kids in Class Seven. They say Class Seven is a strong contender for the trophy. I think Class Two had bad luck with the draw. If I'd known it would come to this, I would have rallied the moms and had a word with the organizers. If you speak up, they at least have to care, you know? Anyway, I'm really sorry I didn't say anything.

Sei's performance isn't bad today. She's quick and agile. Haesoo does not take her eyes off the child. She wants their eyes to meet at some point, and for Sei to know that Haesoo is here.

You know what we all say. To the kids. Just enjoy the game. You don't have to win. But all parents secretly want their kids to win. Just think how sad they'll be if they lose. I'm so worried already.

The woman keeps talking, likewise without taking her eyes off the court. The ball zips back and forth. Each time, a few kids are taken out and sent to the back line.

Where somebody wins, someone else loses, Haesoo replies. The children win, lose, and maybe learn something.

That's not how she really feels. She wants Sei's class to win. If the team wins thanks to Sei's great performance, they might start to treat her differently. Her lowly status among her peers might be elevated a little. Haesoo is aware that Sei is putting everything she has into avoiding the ball for just that reason.

Oh, my God. Aren't you that therapist from TV? Dr. Haesoo Lim? The woman's voice suddenly gets loud.

It is you! I thought you looked familiar. Do you live in this neighborhood? I didn't know you had a child.

Ambush. A nightmare recurring when it's least expected. All the nerves in Haesoo's body start to sing. Blood rushes to her ears. But she isn't carried away by the fear this time. She makes an effort to look straight at her past self, coming back to life. She no longer has the urge to deny that she is that person. If possible, she must enfold that Haesoo in a tight embrace. In the end, that is the only way.

Yes, it is. I'm here to cheer for a young neighborhood friend. I don't have a child, Haesoo answers calmly.

Oh, wow. I can't believe I've run into such a celebrity at a place like this. Who is your little friend? Is she in Class Two? She's a classmate of my Sori.

174

The whistle blows. The referee stops the game and gives the children instructions. It looks like they've been given a warning. The whistle blows again and the game resumes. There are only about half a dozen children left on each side.

Her name is Sei Hwang. There, with the purple headband. Do you see her? Haesoo points at Sei jumping around the court to avoid the ball.

Sei Hwang? Sei? Oh, Sei. You're here for Sei. The woman sounds put off. What has she heard? Does she know that her daughter is ganging up against Sei and bullying her?

Haesoo steels herself so as not to let the accusations and misunderstandings spread inside her like wildfire. A good person, a bad person. Kindness, malice. Haesoo will not label them as such, make snap judgments, and erect a tall fence in between.

The woman says, again in a cheery voice, This must be your day off. At the counseling center, I mean. You're still seeing clients, aren't you? I've always wanted to go some time. When you were on television, the strategies you came up with for people really helped. I really like that show. Too bad you're not on it anymore.

What does this woman want to know? Why do certain questions always translate into rudeness? Haesoo doesn't let anything show. She knows there is no reason to reveal how she feels on the inside, which is close to turmoil right now. She learns a hard truth: sometimes one cannot spit out or swallow words just because one wants to.

I turned out to be lacking in many ways for television, Haesoo says. But thanks for saying so. I'm taking a break from counseling for now. I'm not sure when I'll start again.

Once again, the whistle blows. The game stops. The indistinct chatter quiets and the court freezes. Something has happened on Class Two's side. The children are standing in a circle, neglecting the ball on the ground. The chatter grows louder and louder. Some kids from Class Seven run over to see what's happening.

Hey. Screwed up. Sei. Out. Sei Hwang. Moron. Screwed up. Ass Hwang.

Haesoo catches a few words through the children's shouts. Did something happen to Sei? Are the children giving her a hard time again? The parents, now impatient, come out from under the awning one by one. The referee blows the whistle and gestures at the parents to stay back.

Two more teachers come running. The circle of children steps back slowly to reveal two girls sitting on the court. Sei and a smaller girl. The two get up as the referee instructs, then dust themselves off.

It appears the commotion is over. But it can't be over. Sei, who had been keeping her head down, now lunges at the child. As though she can't take it anymore. As though she cannot let her get away with this. She tosses a fistful of sand and throws herself at the girl. The two children are back on the ground in a cloud of dust. The teachers try to separate them, but it's no use. The two girls roll in a tangle.

Haesoo sees glimpses of Sei amidst the piercing screams and shouts.

Oh, my goodness. What is going on?

Shouldn't we get over there? Who is that girl?

Are they from the same class? It's Class Two, right?

Tension rises in the parents' voices. Shading her face from the sun with both hands, Haesoo steps a little closer to the court. But that is all. She watches. She is watching. What she sees in that moment isn't a tussle that often happens between children. It is the anger that has been plaguing the child for a long time, the loneliness eating her inside, and a final surrender to these overwhelming feelings.

A few parents run toward the court calling their children's names. A few more follow, and then the rest. Haesoo is the only person left standing under the awning.

Dear Juhyun,

How are you? I met that person a few days ago. Euna Noh. The wife of Jeonggi Park. We sat down together at a café and talked like two people with important business to discuss. Can you believe it? Then again, it wasn't really a conversation. That wasn't what I was hoping for, either. I remember thinking, Maybe we can have some semblance of a conversation? Just for a moment? I would be lying if I said that I went into it with no such expectations.

The things I want to say, and the things I need to say—maybe I believed that I would be able to say them all. How naive and foolish of me. Maybe I thought she would hear me out just this once. But I now understand a little of what you said to me back then. Why you told me to meet with the family of that person, and why you said I needed to do it for myself. I'm very slowly starting to see why.

But that's not what I wanted to say in this letter.

Juhyun, I want to talk about something else today.

When that thing happened, when I thought I was caught in the middle of horrendous chaos, I did so many things I should not have done to you. It's late but I want to apologize from the bottom of my heart. I'm not trying to make excuses for myself. Because the mistakes were mine. I made those mistakes. Only now am I seeing what it must have been like for you.

You were so kind to me. So genuine. And I took it all for granted. I should have been more grateful. As a friend, not once did you. In spite of. I was so. I never said

It rains all day long. By the time Haesoo gets to the coffee shop near the vet's office, the hems of her pants are soaked. With every step, water oozes from her wet shoes.

Welcome!

The moment Haesoo steps into the coffee shop, an employee standing by the coffee machine greets her. It's empty in the small café of only four tables. Then Haesoo sees that farther inside is a man getting up to say hello. Sei's father. A man who is raising a ten-year-old girl by himself. The man who is always an omission or a footnote in Sei's stories.

You must be Ms. Haesoo Lim. Nice to meet you. I'm Sei's father. Thank you for taking time out of your busy schedule to meet with me.

Hello. Nice to meet you.

The man's shirt collar is flipped and rolled in on one side. His khaki pants are wrinkled as well. Haesoo catches the sharp smell of mothballs every time he moves. She gathers her dripping umbrella and sits down. The man brings two cups of coffee from the counter.

I thought Sei was joining us, Haesoo says.

Oh, I asked her to wait at the animal hospital, the man answers. I wanted to ask you a few questions alone.

It's almost cool inside the café because of the air conditioning, but the man keeps dabbing sweat from his face with tissue. And then he balls up the damp tissue and holds it in his palm as if he isn't sure what to do with it while he silently cradles the cup containing hot coffee.

In the end, Haesoo has to initiate the conversation. How is Sei? Is she doing better?

Sei? I don't know. When I ask her, she doesn't really tell me. Sometimes she seems okay and other times I have no clue what she's thinking. Maybe I'm not sensitive enough, or maybe she doesn't want to talk to me. It's getting more difficult as she gets older. Oh, I heard you were there at the game that day. You were there.

Yes, I was there. I went because Sei invited me to come. I was standing under the awning with the other parents. Did you speak with the parents of that child?

The man's face falls. He rubs his forehead with a thick, rough hand. He has dark stains around his stubby fingernails, and fresh red scratches on his veiny hand.

I don't know how much Sei has told you, but her mother and I are separated at the moment. And this is a busy time of year at work. So I told Sei's mom about it, but I think she's not able to have a dialogue with the other kid's parents. I don't know why Sei is being treated like a criminal when she is the one who was injured. Honestly, I don't even know how to deal with those people. There's no talking to those people.

Is it serious?

The first time we spoke on the phone, they brought up an investigation and school violence and all that insanity right away. What parent would sit by and listen as someone talks about their kid like she's a monster? As you can see, Sei is not that kind of kid. If she behaved that way, there must have been a reason. Sei would not have done it for no reason.

The man stops for a moment to calm himself. His Adam's apple rises and falls. Haesoo waits.

I think she was bullied at school. This has never happened before. I can imagine how upset she must have been to do something like that. Several times a day I have this urge to just march into that school and give them a piece of my mind. I'm sorry. I didn't ask you here to bellyache.

The man closes his mouth as though to stop the words from leaking out. But after a sip of coffee, he starts talking again.

The other kid's parents are insisting that Sei lunged at her first. If they're so keen on figuring out what happened, what about the fact that their kid bullied my kid first? They talk about that as if it's nothing. I don't understand. I wonder if they're treating her like dirt because her mother's not around. Sei's been so down in the mouth since the separation began. And I don't know how much this incident is going to scar her. Ugh, I'm sorry. I keep . . .

The man wipes at his sweat with the balled-up tissue. He keeps crumpling it up in his hand, smoothing it out again, and crumpling it back up as though it represents how he feels. Haesoo changes the subject.

Has Sei told you about the cat?

What? Cat? Oh, I heard about the cat. She said she rescued a sick cat.

Have you seen the cat? It's at the animal hospital right now.

Not yet. I'm going to see it after. That's also an issue. It's not easy having an animal around the house. It's a small house, and it's hard enough taking care of a kid. Now a sick cat?

There's a lull in the conversation. Haesoo takes a sip of the coffee, now cold. Why did this man ask to meet with her, she wonders. What did he hear from Sei? For Sei's benefit, what is it that she must say to this man? What mustn't she say?

I used to be a therapist. I'm sure Sei told you?

Yes, I know. She told me you're famous. That you come up on the internet.

Sei said that?

Yes.

This comes as a shock. How much does the child know about her? When, where, what, and how did she find out? How much information—some of it being gossip that Haesoo herself has not looked into—has Sei looked up?

Haesoo pushes away the sprawling thoughts and says, Then I'll just be open about it. I once spoke about an actor named Jeonggi Park. On the air. I said that he was a rude, irrespon-sible, incorrigible, and pathetic man. Bad temper, defaulting on loans, getting into fights with colleagues. I thought at the time, how can a man who calls himself an actor live his life like this? A few months later he killed himself. I'm sure you saw it on the news. And I became the person who killed another person. A person who, instead of saving people with words, killed a man with words.

Haesoo's voice is calm. Even-keeled. She is careful to take one step after another away from herself. Self-pity and self-deprecation—she is making an effort not to be swept away by these things. But is that really possible? Is it possible to be cool-headed and speak about this as though it happened to someone else?

It would be a lie to say that she is perfectly fine. She only seems so. She clearly feels something akin to pain. She is aware that it's close to impossible to explain what happened without shame. Without humiliation.

I stopped working in television after that, she continues. I also left the counseling center where I worked for many years. For some time I didn't do any work. I didn't meet anyone, and I didn't stay in touch with anybody. I thought I could go on living like that forever. And then I met Sei. Last spring. In the alley outside my house.

The man is listening. He looks confused, unsure of where she is going with her story. He is hoping beyond hope that she will finally say what he wants to hear. She knows what he's waiting to hear. She knows which words offer validation and comfort. Words that will vanish at the blink of an eye, that evaporate the moment you turn around. It would be easy to offer those words.

But she doesn't intend to. That would not help the man or Sei.

Sei is a good kid, Haesoo says. There's no mistaking that. Sei knows how to look after the cats that live on the streets, and how to become someone's friend. She is a kindhearted, perceptive kid.

The man's eyebrows rise and fall. Thick eyebrows with a gentle downturn of the eyes. Round tip of the nose, slender philtrum. Long, thin lips. She sees Sei's familiar face in his.

But Sei must apologize first for what happened. She has to. Tell her that she must apologize. Teach her how to apologize. Teach her that this is what she needs to do. This is what I want to say to you.

The man looks as if he has hit a dead end. His face falls. He opens his mouth like he's about to say something, but doesn't.

The verdict is reached before the truth is laid out, and a stigma is branded. Haesoo understands this. She also understands that the man seems to feel her response is no different from the parents of the other child. Does he think she doesn't see the pain a child would suffer by apologizing in the midst of such a misunderstanding?

Of course, Haesoo is aware of the man's need to rail against injustice. This is why she doesn't intend to comfort him with gentle, consoling words that pretend to care. She cannot sweep this under the rug and let Sei find herself in a similar conundrum again someday, far in her future. That must not happen.

This matter will be settled if Sei apologizes, she says again. Other problems can be worked out after that. Sei is not going to come out of this damaged. This isn't so big. Sei will learn something important. Help her learn. Help her avoid repeating the same mistakes.

The man sits up straight, as though he's about to say something.

This is a simple matter, Haesoo says. She drives her point in like nails. You just have to go through it step by step. You don't have to complicate it.

∾

A few days pass.

The heat wave that had been lingering begins its retreat. The air coming in through the window feels cool now. The fire abated, is summer ready to move on? For a long time, summers have felt like background noise to Haesoo. But this year, she stood right in the middle of it. She feels now as though she went through the season with nothing to shield her body from the sun.

Late at night, she lies on her sofa watching television.

In a bluish light without the slightest tinge of warmth, some people and figures appear and disappear as they shift shapes. Haesoo has curled up like a cat and stares at the screen. Perhaps what she is staring at isn't the television screen at all. Maybe she's looking at a different time, a different dimension.

A scene comes to mind. Memory is shifting. A thought she had forgotten is coming clear. Moments she has undoubtedly lived through.

She gets off the sofa to shake off the memory. She turns off the television and goes into her study. She sits at her desk for a moment. Every day in the late afternoon, she wrote letters here. For some time now, she has not been writing. She has been learning that she can get through one day, one week, and even one month without writing to anyone. Haesoo realizes that she has now completely lost the urge.

The next morning, she wakes up early.

Turnip is getting out of the hospital today. She gives the house a quick tidying and leaves before ten. She walks to the vet's office. It is overcast. The sun peeks out every now and then through a blanket of low-hanging clouds. Haesoo's strides get increasingly bigger as she hurries ahead.

Sei has arrived before her. A woman is sitting next to her.

Hello, the woman says. Sei's mother. The woman who comes to see the child once a month. She smells faintly like roses. There's a note of alcohol mixed in there as well.

You must be Sei's mother. Nice to meet you, Haesoo says. Her eyes keep catching on the woman's fingers. Long, smooth nails, sparkling gems with a pearly sheen. Iridescent colors and cute patterns.

Oh, heh. The color's a bit strong, isn't it? I run a nail salon. When a new color comes in, I try it on to promote them, but it came out a little busy this time. Maybe that's why the customers didn't show any interest. I'll have to do it over.

The woman spreads her fingers wide to show her, and smiles shyly. Haesoo smiles in return and looks at Sei.

You're here early, Sei, she says sweetly. What happened to your eye? Did you hurt yourself?

Wearing an eyepatch over her right eye, Sei looks sideways up at Haesoo and nods once. She seems glum, or maybe just under the weather. Or maybe she's just clinging to her mother as children her age sometimes do.

Sei, you should answer when a grown-up speaks to you. Don't just nod.

Without looking at her mother, Sei manages to say, I hurt myself, but it's not bad. The doctor said I'll be better in two days.

Haesoo does not ask why she's here instead of at school, or how the brawl was resolved. She talks about other things: cats in the ginkgo tree lot. Haesoo tells Sei that she saw a litter of kittens that look just like Turnip.

Really? You went to see them, Auntie? When?

The child lights up. Haesoo tells her that there's a new, sturdy feeding place made of wood and a little plastic house where the cats can get out of the rain.

I want to go after. Mom, can I go see the kittens with Auntie?

The child deftly receives her mother's permission and flashes Haesoo a smile.

In that moment, the fear binding Haesoo—that they might misunderstand, that her kindness and concern would be misinterpreted—falls away. It is Sei and Sei's mother. Haesoo sees none of the ruthless judgment that has come down on her in Sei and her mother.

What Sei sees is the Haesoo that stands before her. And the girl standing before Haesoo is the same plucky, kind, honest girl she knows. That will not change.

Haesoo sits down. The three of them remain side by side in the exam room, waiting to hear about Turnip's condition.

The vet says in a dry tone, The surgery was delayed because her inflammation did not go down as expected, but the molars were all taken out—top and bottom—and I left the bicuspids. I'll give you some meds to take home, and we'll monitor her for the next few weeks.

Just like that, Turnip is discharged. The nurse goes over every item on the bill with Haesoo and gives her the total.

When Haesoo hands the woman her credit card, the nurse tells her that part of the bill has already been settled.

Really? By whom?

Sei's mother walks up to her and whispers, I wanted to contribute. I would have loved to pay for all of it, but I gave what I could. As a way of saying thanks for looking after Sei.

No, I'm the one who should be grateful. You're adopting Turnip.

Nah, Sei is adopting Turnip. She swore up and down the street that she would be responsible for her, so she'll do a good job. I hope so, anyway.

While Haesoo tries to think of something to say, the woman asks cheerfully, By the way, have you eaten? Would you like to have lunch with us? We could leave Turnip here for a little longer and come back for her.

Haesoo can't think why not. She happily accepts the invitation.

Auntie, guess what? Dodgeball is a really stupid game, the child whispers to Haesoo on the way to the restaurant.

Her mother is a few steps behind, busy on her phone. Haesoo overhears the words *color*, *care*, *appointment*, *customer*, *unhappy*, *service*.

Why, because you lost? Are you sad that you lost?

The child looks up at her and answers, No. That's not it. You practice a lot for many hours, but you lose so quickly. You can spend hours and hours and hours and hours practicing, but you're out the moment the ball hits you.

But practice is just practice. The real game is different from practice, and no one knows how things will turn out in the real game, Haesoo answers.

The child asks again, Then what's the point of practicing? It doesn't help at all.

Do you really think so?

Don't you think so, Auntie?

Is Sei talking about dodgeball, or is she asking about life? Is she asking Haesoo a question, or is she being rhetorical?

Of course not. There's always the next game. It's always the losing side that learns more from it.

Is that true? Haesoo asks herself. Does she really believe this? Haesoo is surprised to find some semblance of comfort in her own words.

∽

To Mr. Hanseong Lee:

Hello, it's Haesoo Lim.

I have made up my mind to accept the counseling center's decision.

I will not be needing the minutes from the final meeting I previously requested. I am likewise dropping the inquiry regarding Minyoung Cho. As for the records of the clients I treated, I would like them to be handled according to the clients' wishes. Please discard anything of mine that remains at the office.

Finally, I would like to express my gratitude to you. I know that you have looked out for me from the beginning. In the time that the counseling center grew, I learned and gained a lot as well. I know that I was very lucky to have worked there. I will keep the happy memories of my time at the counseling center with me for many years to come.

I wish you good health. Thank you.

A few days later, Haesoo meets with her lawyer.

The lawyer looks drained as he greets Haesoo. Haesoo takes a seat across from him in the conference room. It's just as empty as it was at her first visit. Somewhere outside the conference room, phones ring incessantly. The sounds of people talking and walking grow near and then far.

When Haesoo reveals the purpose of her visit, the lawyer falls silent.

It's up to you, he says at last. But I don't think that's a sensible course of action, Dr. Lim. Sweeping it under the rug is not going to resolve the matter. There's no telling what additional problems this might cause later. You're leaving the embers alive.

Haesoo has heard this countless times before. The lawyer spins his pen. The thick, heavy pen balanced on his thumb spins around and around.

The past version of Haesoo would have asked, What problems? What kind of problems will it cause? And the lawyer would have recited a hard-hearted list of everything she has lost, is losing, and will lose. And she would have closed her eyes. She would have blindly backed out of her decision, leaning on the lawyer's advice.

The best thing for cases like this is to act. Make an example out of a few who keep trolling you online and sue them for defamation. It's been a while since the incident, so this won't get too much media attention.

There's a knock on the conference room door. Someone pokes their head in and whispers something. The lawyer nods as if to consent, and waves them away.

No, it's okay. I don't want to take any action. There's no need, Haesoo says.

The lawyer taps the desk lightly with his pen as he holds her gaze. You're really backing down, he seems to say with his eyes. Are you really going to leave yourself open to attacks that you can't foresee now? How are you going to handle all of it then? He seems incredulous that she has come to such a stupid conclusion.

Okay. If that's what you want, there's nothing for me to add. But let me tell you this: you can't trust people. Kindness is only kindness when times are good. Kindness is the first to go when luck changes. Without exception. You need to be prepared for the worst in every case.

The lawyer must be telling the truth. He must be speaking from years of experience frequenting law enforcement and judicial offices like they were his own home, tweaking the scale that balances punishment and crime. Veterans who take logical leaps to fill the gaps. Combatants taking aim at flaws and weaknesses. Fighters hardened by dispute.

But Haesoo has not led a lawyer's life. She therefore cannot think as he does. As a therapist, she has seen wounded and incomparably frail people inside so many of her clients. Confrontation of this nature is impossible without leaning on kindness and empathy.

This faith is perhaps the only thing that remains with Haesoo now. What she has ended up with. What she has not lost. Can she think of it as something she has managed to protect? Can she call it that?

I'll keep that in mind. Thank you, Haesoo answers, and leaves the office.

Later that day, Haesoo and Sei visit the ginkgo tree lot. It's a sunny afternoon. Blooming white clouds float against a brilliant blue sky. It is the heart of summer, but there is an indisputable feeling that the season is slowly receding.

Did you visit your mom at her house? Haesoo asks.

The child answers, Yes, I slept over for two nights. I had pizza and chicken. And there's a room for Turnip there. It's small, but I made it really pretty. And I have a room there, too! It's way bigger than my room now. Do you want to see?

Sei brings up several pictures on her phone.

As Sei chooses pictures to show Haesoo, the corners of the child's eye twitch. Sei does not have to wear the eye patch anymore, but there's still a spot of blood in the white of her eye. It will take longer for the fine scratch on her eyelid to heal as well. Haesoo does not ask Sei when she is moving to her mother's house or bring up what happened at school.

The parents exchanged apologies and compensations that resembled a tug-of-war, resulting in the decision to transfer Sei to another school. But that doesn't mean all the problems have gone away. Something is lying still and holding its breath inside Sei, and there's no telling when it might rise up. This could be a mere truce she's reached through great effort.

The fight Sei faces now is with herself. And when the fight is over, she will know what has been lost or gained. What she was able to protect.

How's your eye feeling? Look. How many fingers do you see? Haesoo waves two fingers in front of Sei like a clown. Old-timey sense of humor. Dumb joke. Stupid things grown-ups did with children when Haesoo was a child.

Two. I can see totally fine, Sei says with a playful scrunch of the nose.

There is no one at the ginkgo tree lot. They find the new feeding place made of wood and a few durable plastic boxes. A huddle of pigeons take to the sky when Haesoo and Sei get too close. A cloud of yellow dust rises.

Wow, it's true! Auntie, this looks really good! It's very sturdy! Do you think Maru Mom did it?

Sei is right. A tag is firmly affixed to one corner of the feeding place, bearing a name, a phone number, and a warning that there will be legal consequences if anyone removes it. It's Maru Mom's number.

Sei examines the clean setup of kibble, water, and plastic homes, and starts searching for the kittens. She looks around the lot's open spaces first, then around the thick shrubbery, and even around the back of the ginkgo tree.

Auntie!

Haesoo goes over to Sei, who looks up at her and points. There is another ginkgo tree behind this one. Because the two trees stand in a straight line, they have always looked like one tree. The tree in the back is much bigger and greener than the one in front.

There are two trees! You didn't know either, right?

You're right. I thought it was one tree.

Haesoo looks up at the ginkgo tree, surprised to learn that the green leaves that have often caught her eye in truth belong to the tree behind it. Strangely moved to learn that the stuff of fiction exists in the real world.

If everything is leaning on something else, what is she leaning on? she thinks. And what is leaning on her? Names of certain people, moments that stayed with her come to mind.

At last, two kittens emerge from the shrubbery. One white kitten and one that looks just like Turnip. Sei scoops out some of the canned food on a flat rock. The cats come one after the other, lap up every last bit of the food, and prowl around Sei and Haesoo.

Sei and Haesoo stay in the lot for a while. They watch the cats try to hunt pigeons. They watch the cats slowly and thoroughly lick their paws as they bask in the sun. They watch the cats retreat into the plastic boxes for a nap.

A peaceful afternoon, a moment of stillness, a pause.

But even in this stillness, time continues on. The last blaze of summer will give way to cool winds, then snow. Time will advance without rest. That cannot be avoided. And like all living things, Haesoo has a duty to live through this phase, then the next, and so on.

Is her long standstill finally ending? Is she beginning to stretch her limbs and take a breath? Haesoo is surprised by her own thoughts.

Sei, you know I used to be a famous therapist, right? You know Auntie was in the news and on TV, Haesoo asks as they leave the lot. Sei dawdles to say goodbye to the kittens, and catches up to her with a cursory, I know. Without slowing down or looking back at Sei, Haesoo keeps talking. About the beginning and end of the incident that she caused, the period of recovery she had to get through, the season she had to endure. She tells her about the moments that the child probably already knows about, but will never fully understand. About the long, dark night that this unsuspecting child will have to confront.

Huh? Did you say something, Auntie? I couldn't hear you, Sei asks as she runs alongside Haesoo, a cloud of dust rising in her wake.

I said thank you, Haesoo says. I'm glad you're around, Sei.

Sei is coming on Saturday.

The day begins by threatening rain, but now the skies are clearing up. Haesoo opens all the windows in her house and puts the radio on low. Then she fetches two folding tables from storage, one at a time. They're large and heavy enough that it requires two hands to move them. She dusts the tables and wipes them down. Then she goes into her study to make space for the tables.

Haesoo sorts through the dizzying piles on her desk. She returns with a large plastic bag for things she no longer has a use for. Colorful paper clips and binder clips. Frayed and creased notepads and calendars. Pamphlets and reports. Overdue tax notices and bills. Business cards and postcards from who knows whom, where, or when. Pens that don't work. Old memos. Books she hasn't opened in a long time.

Then she collects the few letters she has written that she has yet to dispose of—letters she wrote once a day, letters she never finished or sent. The words she chose after an agonizing search. She sweeps them into the plastic bag without a second thought. The desk is clean. She goes through the drawers and bookshelves while she's at it. So many things she swore she would find a use for, things she thought she would need at some point, things she thought she'd sooner die than throw away—she does not think twice about them now.

Space opens up inch by inch. Sweat trickles down her back. Outside the window, the roars of cicadas ebb and flow. The cramped, stuffy room looks much bigger once it's cleaned out. She sets up the two folding tables side by side in the middle of the room and checks their evenness. Then she brings a chair with a back and adjusts the height.

Haesoo sits in the chair and takes a deep breath.

Then she carefully looks around at everything Sei will see, hear, and feel. Haesoo is determined not to leave anything to chance. The child has opened up to her through much difficulty, and she will not let her shut down again. She can at least make sure nothing in the environment will get on Sei's nerves. Haesoo's eyes slowly sweep her familiar, yet new room.

Sei arrives before two in the afternoon. She is dressed up. Haesoo finds her at the gate just as she is taking out several bags of trash.

Here. Mom told me to give you this, Sei says, offering the paper bag as soon as she sees Haesoo. It contains a roll cake and handmade chocolates. The child places her shoes neatly by the door and comes inside. Then, instead of sinking back into the couch with her legs drawn up as she normally does, she sits on the edge with her back straight. She appears to have received instructions from her mother, which she is following to a tee.

Sei, have you had lunch? Haesoo asks, pulling the roll cake out of the bag. Do you want to try some of this with me?

I had lunch with Mom, thank you. The cake is for you, Ms.

Did you just call me "Ms."? What happened to "Auntie," Sei?

A bashful smile appears on Sei's face as she answers, I don't know. Mom told me to call you that from now on.

Haesoo tells her that there is no need for formalities. And she means it. Because Sei and Haesoo aren't meeting for the first time. Unlike so many clients Haesoo has treated over the years, they don't need to refer to each other by honorifics and slowly get to know each other from the start. But that doesn't mean she understands Sei perfectly. Inside Sei lives a side of her that Haesoo has yet to meet. There are parts of Sei that Haesoo cannot predict or even fathom. She is a living, changing thing, like the sun that rises and sets, like the seasons that come and go. As long as the child is living, Haesoo will never be able to keep up with her. To know her completely.

They sit together in the wide-open living room for some time before Haesoo takes Sei into her study.

Sei seems a little nervous. Haesoo pulls out the chair and lets Sei take her time settling in. Haesoo studies the room one more time for the level of light and temperature. Then she goes into the kitchen and returns with two glasses of orange juice. She sets them down on the table and brings over a box of tissues and several pieces of chocolate.

Haesoo cannot seem to sit down. She realizes that she is trying to avoid that moment. For years she repeated this process ad nauseam—does the process mean something different to her now? Have the pride and privilege she used to associate with her profession disappeared completely?

Sipping her orange juice, Sei watches Haesoo. She cautiously follows her with worried, inquisitive eyes.

Oops, Auntie forgot to wipe the table. Give me just a moment.

Just as Haesoo heads for the door, Sei interjects, It's okay. I can wipe it!

Sei wipes the table with her sleeve before Haesoo can stop her. Then she flashes a playful grin. Haesoo finally surrenders and sits down. Just as she was when she started this work a long time ago, she is scared and nervous. Eager and curious.

Haesoo used to sit alone in this room and write letters. In the ruins, cut off from others, she believed that she was using a certain language, certain words to wage war against the world outside. And she has learned nothing from it. She did not win or lose. Just as time passes whether or not one assents or disapproves, she only lived through another season.

That much she can tell the child. If she wants. If the child requests it. She will wait for that time. And listen as closely as she can in the interim.

Haesoo sits up, shoulders back and back straight. Sei meets her eye.

All right, then. We can talk about anything. Don't be nervous. You can say anything you want to say, Haesoo says. Sound good?

Don't be nervous? Haesoo is obviously the nervous one. Sei smiles shyly, But Haesoo can also see a serious look setting in. Sei must have chosen a story to tell Haesoo. Has she picked a secret to reveal?

Ready?

I've been ready for a long time.

Haesoo runs her hands over the table's surface. She cannot remember when, where, and why she bought these plain tables, but it is enough. Sticks and stones. There is no better place than this table to put up a tower of sticks and stones that may topple at the flick of a finger.

Sei begins her story.

ABOUT THE AUTHOR

KIM HYE-JIN is an award-winning author from Daegu, South Korea. She won the JoongAng Literature Award in 2013 for *Central Station*, the Shin Dong-yup Prize for Literature in 2018 for *Concerning My Daughter*, and the Daesan Literary Award in 2020 for *The Work of No. 9*. She was also the Special Award Laureate of the 4th Lee Hochul Literary Prize for Peace in 2020.

ABOUT THE TRANSLATOR

JAMIE CHANG is a literary translator. Her translation of Cho Nam-joo's *Kim Jiyoung, Born 1982* was longlisted for the 2020 National Book Awards for Translated Literature. She is the recipient of the Daesan Foundation Translation Grant and a three-time recipient of the Literature Translation Institute of Korea Grant.